THE CAD AND DAD

THE CAD AND DAD

SOUTHERN DISCOMFORT BOOK ONE

IAN O. LEWIS

EDITED BY
ANN ATTWOOD

PROLOGUE
CARY

"Well, I'll be damned." I grinned, eyeing the line of hot young guys waiting to enter Legends. I'd moved to Raleigh a month ago, and I'd finally gotten around to checking out the nightclub. It wasn't much to look at on the outside, but the dudes in line most certainly were. "Twinks," I sighed. They never want more than a night or two of simple sex, and that's why they are so perfect. At their age, they are unsophisticated, and demand nothing more than to give and take pleasure.

I was the oldest guy in line, but that didn't bother me one bit. It meant less competition. What most guys my age didn't understand was that if you kept yourself in reasonable shape, younger men flocked to you. When they saw me, all they saw was a mature man willing to buy them a few drinks, perhaps dance to a few songs, and they knew I had the experience to get them off, no strings attached.

"Hi, Vic." A pair of hot young studs greeted the bouncer, bypassing the line altogether. The bouncer was a muscular black man wearing a simple black suit and a red bowtie. One twink turned back and locked eyes with me. He was gorgeous, with bright-blue eyes, dark curly hair cut short, and a bubble butt you could bounce quarters off of. He reached down, adjusted his package, and winked at me.

"Good to see you guys." The hulking bouncer unclipped the velvet rope to let them in. "Here," he handed them what looked like red tickets. "Your first drink is on the house."

The dude who eyed me pecked the bouncer on the cheek and strolled into the club.

"You're going to love me, baby." I murmured, then prayed the twink didn't find someone else before I made it to the entrance of the club. He was exactly my type. The kid didn't look stupid, which meant he could probably hold up his end of a conversation. Plus, the way he grabbed his junk and winked meant I wouldn't have to do much work persuading him to come home with me. Not that I ever struggled to get twinks in my bed. Hell, I'd never dated anyone older than thirty in my life.

"Your ID, sir." The bouncer asked, and I handed it to him along with a twenty-dollar bill. He pocketed the money, undid the velvet rope, and ushered me inside. After walking down a long, dark corridor, a security guard opened a door. Bright lights and thumping beats greeted me when I brushed past him.

"Yes, I'm home again." I grinned, eyeing the packed dance floor filled with shirtless, muscular men. "It's magic time."

I scanned the room, hoping to find the twink I'd seen outside. It wasn't that I was solely looking for a one-night stand, though that would be perfectly acceptable. What I wanted was to worship at the altar of youth, to feel his taut skin underneath my hands. Men my age didn't know what they were missing. These young guys weren't looking for anything serious. All they wanted was someone to listen to their hopes and dreams, and I was all ears if they turned me on.

"Hey."

I felt a hand on my shoulder and spun around to see the hot guy who'd cut through the line.

"You are a sight for sore eyes," I winked, and the twink bit his lower lip. "My name is Cary." I held out my hand, and the youngster stared at it for a moment before shaking it.

"Sam," He replied, and I felt his finger working the tender skin of my palm. His bright blues bored into mine, and a white smile split his face. His parents must have spent a fortune at the dentist office, because his teeth were blindingly perfect. "I've never seen you before."

"That's because I'm new to Raleigh. Just moved here a month ago from New York." I said. "I'm sure you don't need reminding of this, but you are the hottest guy in the room. Can I buy you a drink?"

Sam's cheeks grew pink, and in that moment I knew two things about him. First, underneath his good looks, he was shy. Second, he was as attracted to me as I was to him.

"Yes, please."

———

Instead of heading straight to the bar, Sam took my hand and led me to an outdoor patio. Speakers piped in the music playing on the dance floor, and groups stood around in circles. He took my arm and strolled us to a dark corner. I spied a tiki bar across from us.

"What are you drinking?" I asked, while Sam leaned against the wooden fence.

"I'm a cheap date," Sam grinned. "A beer will be fine." He pressed his palm against my chest for a long moment, and my mouth watered. Damn, I loved the sound of his voice. It was slower than the New York accent I was used to, each word gliding into the next.

"Be right back." I reluctantly stepped away, then headed toward the bar. Sam was exactly what I wanted. A potential fling where we enjoyed each other for a time, then we'd graciously exit each other's lives. I had no interest in setting up housekeeping with him, or having a mini-van parked in the driveway of a two-story house in the suburbs.

There was a line at the bar, and while I was waiting for the bartender, I noticed myself in the mirror behind the rows of liquor bottles.

I might be forty-nine years old, but I'm still the hottest dude in the club. A grin spread across my cheeks, and I winked at my reflection. That's when I noticed two guys my age standing behind me in line, holding hands. Each sported a gold band on their ring fingers, and neither of them appeared thrilled to be here. Hell, they looked downright exhausted.

Their version of happiness was the opposite of mine. No strings, only fun and romance for a short while until I move on to another adventure.

"What'll you have, sir?" The bartender asked, snapping me out of my thoughts.

"Two IPAs." I replied, and while he filled the pint glasses, I thought about what my life could've been like.

Going to the bar once a month with a husband, no excitement, nothing fun. Holding a hand mottled with age spots. And sex, that was probably on a monthly schedule, too.

I paid the bartender and grabbed the pint glasses from the bar, then headed toward my destiny. Nothing boring or settled about a twink who looked like Sam.

I handed him a glass, and he sipped the beer. An adorable, foamy mustache formed on his upper lip, and I wanted to lick it off. Sam patted the bench built into the wall and hopped up on it.

"Sit."

I did as instructed, leaving an inch between us, so I didn't seem too handsy. Sam scooted closer to me, and his thigh felt hot against mine.

"You never told me your name." He said, and he laid his hand on my thigh. I had told him, but perhaps he'd been distracted.

"Cary. Cary Lancaster."

"Why the hell would you leave New York to live in little old Raleigh?" Sam's touch was making my cock firm up. I stared into his blue eyes for a moment before answering. Jesus, the kid radiated innocence, but the way he was touching me was the exact opposite. Sam knew what he wanted, and I couldn't wait to oblige.

"I sold my business and decided I wanted a new adventure. So I closed my eyes, pointed at a map, and my finger landed on Raleigh." I grinned. "If it doesn't work out, I can always move back. Tell me about you, Sam. Are you in school?"

"Yes." He downed his beer, then wiped his lips with the back of his hand. "UNC-Chapel Hill. Working on my Phd in film studies. I want to move to LA and make movies." Sam took my pint glass out of my hand and downed the contents. Shit, just my luck. The kid was a drunk.

"Do you want another..."

"No more beer." Sam stood, pressing his palm against my thigh as he did, then leaned forward and whispered. "Let's get out of here. Do you live close by?"

"On Fayetteville Street, at the..."

Sam laid one hand on my mouth, and with the other, he pressed down on my erect cock.

"Stop talking. You want what I want, so take me home with you now."

CHAPTER 1

CARY

"This is so beautiful," I said over the disco diva, wailing through the car speakers. The mountains were stunning. "I should've moved to North Carolina years ago."

Sam placed his hand on the back of my neck and I saw him grin through the rear-view mirror. Then, without warning, he snatched the cigar out of my lips and tossed it out of the car.

"Hey!"

"There's no smoking at my dad's place, and trust me, he can smell smoke for days afterward." Sam said, then stretched his arms over his head and yawned. "What kind of car is this again? It's amazing."

"Rolls Royce Cullinan. It arrived a week ago, and this is my first time taking it out on the road." It was royal blue, and a convertible. "I thought you said your Pop wouldn't be there."

"He's not. Dad's going to the beach house in Nags Head to get some work done." Sam patted my thigh. "You two wouldn't get along."

"Hey, that's not fair. Nobody hates Cary Lancaster." I laughed, then noticed a sign by the side of the road for the Biltmore Estate. It was the largest home in North America, built by the Vanderbilt family. "You must be rich, living around here."

"I'm not rich, my dad is. Writing bestselling novels made him a fortune. He insists I pay my own way, which includes college." Sam said.

"That doesn't sound terribly fair." I murmured. "If you've got the resources you should help your kids out."

"Actually, I'm glad he didn't. It's made me stronger. I've paid for school through scholarships and by being a teaching assistant." Sam sighed. "The one perk I get is being able to stay at his homes at the beach and here in the mountains."

"My family was in publishing. Your Pop and I would have a lot to talk about. Maybe one day we can meet." I said, and Sam giggled.

"No, you don't want to do that. I mean, my father is awesome, and a brilliant writer, but he's totally not your type." Sam drawled.

"One of the fabulous things about me is I don't have a type." I replied, and Sam laughed.

"Cary, my dad is over thirty. I think that means he's not your type."

I turned my head in his direction and stuck out my tongue.

"Please, Cary. I've done my research online. You're notorious for dating younger guys." Sam said, and I felt his fingers playing with the hair on the back of my head.

"Spying on me, huh?" I stuck my tongue out at him again.

"You've got a reputation. Nothing wrong with that. Lucky for you, I'm addicted to Daddies, especially ones who drive Rolls Royces." Sam said.

"You're dating me for my money, huh?" I laughed, not

meaning it. Apparently, he came from money too, so I wasn't too worried he was a gold digger.

"Of course not, silly. But you never date guys over thirty. It's a fact, and it's not a big deal."

"Sam, it just so happens that dudes over thirty don't want to date me, smartass." I giggled at my lie, and Sam leaned over and pecked me under the ear.

"Make the next left, slowly. You'll see a metal gate. When we get there, you'll need to punch in the code." Sam said, and I did as instructed. Moments later, Sam told me the code, and I punched it in. The gate swung open, and I drove up an asphalt driveway. "It's two miles until we get to the house."

Thick forest surrounded us, and the air appeared green thanks to the thick canopy overhead. "Have I told you how sexy you look in that tank top, how I get hard just staring at your pecs?"

Sam laughed. "Yes, you have. Many, many times."

A stunning three-story house, which resembled a ski lodge, came into view. It was constructed of wood and stone, with large glass windows covering most of the front.

"Wow," I murmured. "It's the perfect mountain retreat."

"Oh, yes, of course it is. My Dad is a perfectionist, and wouldn't have it any other way. You know, he didn't make his fortune from writing until I was in middle school. Every weekend he and my other dad would drive us up here to…"

"Your other dad?" I interrupted, then Sam pulled his phone out and pointed it at the house. A hidden garage door inched open.

"They divorced after I graduated. I'm adopted." He said. "Pull into the garage."

I did as he told me, then shut off the engine. "Do they along? Your Pops, I mean."

"Oh, yeah. They're still friends, kind of. My other

literary agent." Sam stepped out of the car, and I popped the trunk so we could get our bags. "They share the house here and at the beach. The divorce was very civilized. Now my other dad, his name is Brian, lives in New York most of the time. They share a penthouse there, too."

Huh. I wondered if I knew his father, Brian. Until five years ago, I owned a successful publishing house before selling it to Simon & Schuster. I opened the glove box and snuck a few cigars into my shirt pocket.

"So, what are we going to do with ourselves for the next two days?" I asked, then noticed a hot tub and a swimming pool in the backyard through a window. Thank God I'd brought my swim trunks, though I hoped I wouldn't actually have to wear them. Sam and I had fooled around, but we'd never done much more than getting each other off. This weekend, I wanted to take our sexual relationship to the next level.

Sam strolled over to me, dropped our bags, then wrapped his arms around my neck. "Anything you want, as long as we're naked." He nuzzled my ear, and my cock thickened.

"Is your pool heated? If so, why don't we go for a swim." It was chilly here in the mountains, compared to Raleigh.

"Yes, it is." Sam winked, then pulled his red tank top over his head. "No swimsuits are required, Daddy."

I bit my lower lip and heard a growl deep in my chest. It turned me on when he called me Daddy. "Sounds like a plan." I picked up our bags. "Let's go inside and then get out of these clothes."

"Hey, those aren't cigars in your pocket, are they?" Sam sked, reaching into his shorts and pulling out a set of keys. He lled over to a door and opened it. "I'm not joking about He hates smoking, and can smell it from a mile away."

he doesn't have a problem with you bringing men

here for sexy times, huh?" I leered at Sam, and walked past him through the door.

"He doesn't know everything I do." Sam slapped my ass. "Or everyone I do it with. He's kind of conservative about sex and stuff."

We walked through a narrow corridor, then Sam opened a door and the sunshine streaming in the many windows nearly blinded me.

"Let me run outside and turn the heat on in the pool, then I'll give you the grand tour." Sam pecked me on the cheek, then opened a tall glass door that opened onto the backyard. I watched him for a second, bent over while pushing some buttons by the Olympic-sized pool.

"I'm going to fuck you stupid in that pool, boy." I murmured, then ogled my surroundings. The kitchen reminded me of a set on a cooking show. Everything was either polished chrome or wood, and I could only imagine how much effort it would take to keep the windows clean. Shiny pots and pans hung from a rack attached to the ceiling, and a mini-greenhouse was attached to one of the windows, filled with herbs.

"I'm back." A shirtless Sam took me by the arm. "Just leave the bags here."

He led me out of the kitchen, then gestured around a room they must have copied from a ski lodge. "This is the living room, perfect for intimate encounters in front of the fireplace. And that fluffy white rug has seen plenty of action." Sam winked, then unbuttoned the top button of his shorts.

The fireplace was big enough to stand in, and there was a stack of logs on both sides. Sam pulled his shorts down, then leered at me.

"Your pants, Cary. Take them off now."

Suddenly it was quiet, almost too quiet, and the sound my zipper being pulled down filled the air. I stepped c them and draped them across an enormous white leather couch. Then, I unbuttoned my shirt and stood in front of Sam. Normally I went commando, but had chosen to wear tight, black briefs.

"As much as I want to make love to you in front of the fireplace, there are way too many windows." I grinned. Tonight would be perfect for playing in front of the fire, but it was still late afternoon, and I felt exposed.

"Fine," Sam laughed. "Though I never took you for the shy type." He held out his hand for me to take, then led me up a wide staircase with a plush crimson runner. When we got to the top, we took a left. "That is the master bedroom, which is off-limits." Sam pointed at one of the rooms. We turned another corner, and he opened a door. "This is where the magic happens, Daddy." Sam giggled, then raced over to a king-sized bed and threw himself on top of it, spread-eagled in his underwear. He patted the mattress next to him and winked.

"Wait," I held a hand up. "As much as I want to join you, I brought a couple of bottles of champagne. Let me stick them in the refrigerator now, or they won't be cold enough later."

Sam reached into his briefs and licked his lips. "Don't take too long, Cary."

I bit my lower lip, wanting to jump in bed next to him, but as much as I loved sex, I also loved a little bit of romance. "Be right back, stud." I spun around and raced out of the room.

When I found our bags, I unzipped mine and pulled out the bottles. As I did, I noticed my reflection in one of the glass windows. "Damn it, I need to go to the gym more often." I muttered, then sucked in my stomach.

I strolled into the kitchen, placed the bottles on the wood island in the center of the room and opened the fridge. "Wow, it s everything you could want." The fridge was fully stocked. I ed a couple of metal racks built into it for wine bottles, and spun around to grab the champagne. Standing in the kitchen doorway were a man and a woman clutching each other, and I yelped in surprise.

"Who the fuck are you, and what are you doing in my house?"

CHAPTER 2
THATCH

"I'm uh..."

Before the stranger could answer, my sister Celia Mae yanked a butcher knife out of the wooden block. "Mister, I'm fixin' to change you from a rooster to a hen if you don't put your hands in the air and face the wall."

My heart was pounding so hard I wondered if I'd die the way my daddy did from a stroke. "You'd best listen to her. Now shut the refrigerator door and do as she told ya."

The man backed up a foot and slowly shut the door, then faced us, his hands covering his crotch. All he had on was a pair of black drawers and a red and white striped shirt unbuttoned to the waist.

"Hands in the air, asshole." Celia Mae barked, and the stranger did as he was told.

"Is this your house?" The man's voice trembled. "If it is, you should..."

"Shut it." I glared at him, and his dark eyes dropped to floor. "Don't say another word, or Celia Mae will make on her threat, and trust me, she'll enjoy it." I growled, then pulled my phone out. "Calling 911 on your ass."

"Please, I'm a friend of your son." The words tumbled out of the man's mouth. "I promise, I..."

"My nephew is in Chapel Hill right now. What the hell are you doing breaking into my brother's house? Are you high on crack or something? Because you sure look fucked up." By the sound of my sister's voice, she was enjoying this.

"I swear, Sam..."

"Shut up!" I yelled, then called 911. "Not another... yes, this is Thatch Fuller, and me and my sister caught an intruder in my house. It's at 2729 Morrison Way."

"I'm dating your son, Sam. He asked me here for the weekend, and he's upstairs right now. I swear on everything holy I'm not a burglar." The man's dark eyes bored into mine.

"You're what?!" I gasped, realizing with dismay he was telling the truth. "Oh shit, sorry officer, um, I think there's been a mistake. A few of them, actually." I disconnected the call and my jaw dropped. "You can't be dating Sam."

The man's hands dropped down, covering his crotch. Then he shook his head and had the gall to wink at me. "My dating your son isn't meant to be bad news, Mr. Fuller."

"Fuck my life." Sam stalked into the kitchen wearing a blue towel wrapped around his waist. "Aunt Celia Mae put the knife down. He's with me, I swear. Dad, you told me you were going to the beach house to write this weekend."

"I did, but I changed my mind because they're predicting storms on the coast." I replied, then a disturbing thought crossed my mind. Like, how often was Sam bringing strange men to my house?

"Well now, this is an awkward family moment." The strange man chuckled, and it almost sounded like he was enjoying it.

"Seriously guys," Sam stretched out a hand toward the man.

"You really think a burglar would only be in his underwear?" My son giggled. "This is funny, if you think about it."

"Jesus, Sam, how the hell were we to know who he was?" My sister slid the knife back into the block. "There are a lot of crazy things going on in this world, and neither of us knows the man."

Sam busted out laughing, clutching his stomach. "I'm sorry." Tears streamed from his eyes. "I should have told you I was bringing someone here." He bent over giggling, and when he straightened up, his towel slipped, then he spun around before flashing us.

"Haven't seen this much of the boy since he was potty trained." Celia Mae drawled.

"Sam, I'm sorry too. I should've told you I'd canceled my weekend at the beach." I sighed, then sat on one of the stools surrounding the kitchen island. "Well, here we are." I waved at Sam's friend. "I'm Thatch, Sam's father. This is my sister, Celia Mae."

The man grabbed a cooking towel off the counter and dangled it in front of his crotch. "Nice to meet you. My name is Cary Lancaster."

"Dad, um, we've been going out for a couple of weeks. I thought I'd mentioned it on our last phone call. We decided since you wouldn't be here, we'd relax by the pool, and I was going to take Cary to the Biltmore Estate for the tour." Sam leaned against the counter, one hand holding his towel in place. "It was a spur-of-the-moment thing."

"Yeah, sure." Celia Mae muttered, then blew a wisp of her bleached-blonde hair off her face.

"Sam, does Cary have a robe he can put on?" I asked. "You might want to put one on too."

Cary held his hand up. "You know what? I think I'll take off so you three can enjoy a little family time."

Sam grimaced. Shit, my boy was all grown up, and in his eyes I'd just messed up what he hoped would be a romantic getaway. But, Jesus, the guy had to at least be my age. What the hell did he see in Cary? Didn't matter, because Sam would be pissed at me if I didn't make the older man feel welcome.

"No, I won't hear of it. Plus, Sam will be madder than a wet hen if you leave, and he'll blame me." I sighed, then forced myself to smile. "Celia Mae and I will drive into Asheville and go to that expensive supermarket, you know, the organic one. You and my boy can get um, cleaned up, and maybe take a dip in the pool. We'll be gone two or three hours." I glanced at my sister, and she had the same forced smile plastered on her face that I did. "Sorry about calling the cops on you, Cary."

"Don't be sorry, it must have shocked you to see me rifling through your refrigerator in my underwear. You were actually quite butch." Cary winked at me, and I felt a blush creeping up my neck. If he thought calling me butch was buttering me up, he had another think coming. "Though your sister and her knife scared the hell out of me."

"I wasn't exactly butch." Something about this man pissed me off. "Celia Mae took these fighting classes from some Israeli guy. What was that called again?" I turned my head and noticed she had her fists balled up.

"Krav Maga." She grinned. "Nobody's going to mess with me."

All of us laughed, but it wasn't a joyful sound. It was too awkward for that.

"Since we've gotten this little family drama sorted out, I'm going upstairs to grab my things and then I'll hit the road." Cary walked over to Sam and pecked him on the cheek. "Call me."

Sam's head and shoulders drooped.

"Well, I declare, don't be so hasty, Cary." Celia Mae walked past him, opened the fridge and pulled out a tupperware container. "You can't go without tasting my pecan pie. It's my Mama's recipe, and it's absolutely sinful." She placed the container on the counter and pulled a knife from the block. "We are all adults here, so there's no need for drama. Why don't we all stay and enjoy a peaceful weekend together. Thatch is working on his next novel, and I've got paperwork to catch up on. Sam, you and Cary can relax by the pool, and my big brother and I will stay out of your way. There's no reason anyone needs to go."

"Yeah, I can handle it. We're all adults." A smile stretched across Sam's face.

Shit. I'd rather Cary left, but I'd look like a shitheel if I asked him to go. I threw my hands up in the air and said through clenched teeth, "Fine. All four of us will have a relaxing weekend together."

Cary eyed all of us warily, then walked over to Sam and placed the hand not clutching the kitchen towel on his shoulder. "Let's get dressed and go to the Biltmore. I love big houses."

Sam jumped up and down for a moment, and his towel threatened to fall off again. "Thanks! You won't be sorry, Cary!"

———

Once Sam and Cary went upstairs, I turned to my sister and scowled. "The next time that man says he wants to leave, just hush your mouth."

She placed a slice of pecan pie on a saucer and slid it in front of me. "Accept the fact that your son is dating Cary. He's an adult, Thatch. You either embrace it, or he'll run in the opposite direction."

"But, why does he have to be so damned old?" I sighed,

then decided I needed more than pie. I walked over to the fridge, reached into the freezer and pulled out a quart of vanilla ice cream. I'd just eat my shitty attitude away.

"He's not ancient, you know." Celia Mae giggled. "Though bless his heart, it looks a little desperate to date someone young enough to be your child. He's gotta be our age, if not a year or two older."

"And that accent." I muttered. "I love New York, but lord, people speak too fast there."

"Well, we can't change who Sam is attracted to, though I wonder if he's having Daddy issues." Celia Mae pulled the ice-cream scoop out of a drawer and handed it to me.

"Daddy issues? He's got two of us." I grumbled, referring to my ex-husband, Brian. Both of us were very involved in Sam's life. Celia Mae bit her lip, then replied.

"Give him a chance, Thatch. If Sam likes him, that's good enough for me."

CHAPTER 3

CARY

"Bye, Dad. Cary and I should be back in time for dinner. Are you cooking, or do you want us to pick something up on the way home?" Sam called out as we walked through the kitchen. Both his father and aunt stared at us for a moment, and I'd swear I saw loathing in Thatch's eyes.

"No, that's um, we're going to Asheville in an hour. We'll pick up something there. How does Mexican sound?" Thatch asked, then his elbow sent a saucer crashing to the floor. "Shit." He grumbled.

"Dad, that sounds great." Sam grabbed my arm and pulled me toward the garage. Halfway down the corridor, he stopped me and whispered. "I told you so."

"Told me what?"

"That you and he wouldn't get along. Dad is very particular about stuff, and he's probably wondering why I'm going out with, well, someone your age." Sam shook his head, then began speeding toward the garage again.

"Hey, I just thought of something." I said, racing to keep up with him. He was practically sprinting down the hallway. "Where's your dad's car, or your aunt's? There weren't any other cars in the garage when we got here."

"They probably were out running errands and when they returned parked their cars in the driveway. Either that, or..." Sam opened the door to the garage, where there were now three vehicles. "... they truly thought a burglar robs houses in his underwear and drives a Rolls Royce. God, old people are nuts."

That hurt. "We're probably the same age. I'm forty-nine. How old is Thatch?"

"Fifty-one. Sorry, I said that." Sam winked at me and opened the passenger door. "You aren't old."

"Asshole," I mumbled under my breath, then got behind the wheel and fastened the seatbelt. "So, do people live at the Biltmore Estate now? The only Vanderbilts I know, well, knew, were Gloria and Anderson Cooper."

"You've met Anderson Cooper?" Sam stared at me with his eyes wide open.

"Shut your mouth before a bug flies in it." I chuckled. "Yes, I've met him several times. I lived in New York, remember? We were at some of the same parties, that kind of thing."

"He's dreamy." Sam sighed. "Oh, and nobody lives there except a few of the staff. It's too big for real people. The Vanderbilt's would still have money if they hadn't built the place."

"Well, let's hit the road."

"Damn." Sam sighed. "I wished we'd seen that sign when we passed it on the way to Dad's house earlier."

The Biltmore Estate was closed for a private function. "Well, I guess we'll head back. Your dad and aunt are gone by now.

Maybe we can have a little afternoon delight." I squeezed Sam's knee.

Fifteen minutes later, we pulled into the garage and unfortunately for us, his family was still there.

"Shit," Sam muttered, then got out of the car.

We said nothing as we walked down the long corridor back into the house. I wished I'd gone home instead of staying here, but the look on Sam's face had kept me from leaving. Nothing against his family, but I'd come here for some action, and having them around was a definite boner killer.

"Hey, why are you guys back so soon?" Thatch asked when we entered the kitchen.

"Barn door is open, Cary." Celia Mae nodded at me, and I didn't know what she was talking about. I must have looked confused, because Sam whispered in my ear, "Your zipper is down."

"Oh." I pulled it up and grinned at our hosts. "The Biltmore was closed for a private function. So, here we are."

"Yes, here you are." Thatch sighed. I swear the man hated me.

"Well, we were about to run into town. You two can help pick out what we're eating for supper." Celia wiped her hands on a kitchen towel, then grabbed her brown leather purse off the counter.

"You don't have to join us if you don't want to." Thatch said, rising to his feet. Then his eyebrows drew together for a moment. "We haven't spent a lot of time together recently, Sam. Let's all go. I want to visit that Mexican grocery store next to the River Arts District."

Swear to God, the man changed his mind because he didn't want Sam and I to be alone. But I'd agreed to stay for the weekend, and Thatch was the host.

"Fine." I said, holding my hands out. "A family outing. What could be better?"

———

"This is one fancy-ass car you've got, Cary." Celia Mae drawled from the backseat. I hadn't wanted to drive, but they wanted to know what it was like to be in a Rolls Royce.

"I can't wait to tell my friends at school about it." Sam patted my thigh, then I backed into a parking space in front of a pottery studio and shut off the ignition.

"You guys aren't poor," I laughed. "Get your dad to buy you one. Totally worth the cash."

"No, no, no." Thatch said, stepping out of the car. "Houses are my luxuries. You lose half the value of a car just by driving it off the lot."

"Not with a Rolls Royce." I clicked the button on my key fob and the doors all locked. "An antique Rolls can sell for hundreds of thousands of dollars."

"I'd be too afraid of wrecking it," Celia Mae said as we stepped onto the sidewalk, then she loudly whispered, "Look at the woman with the purple hair."

I pointed at her and she elbowed me. "Don't point. That's rude. But I swear to God her pants are so tight you can see her religion."

All of us stared for a moment, then Sam cracked up laughing. "Damn it, Aunt Celia Mae, we can't take you anywhere."

Thatch cleared his throat. "Chapala Tienda is right around the corner. Who's in the mood for tamales?" He asked, then strolled ahead of us.

The sun was drooping overhead, and wisps of orange and violet clouds streaked the sky. "I must confess that North Carolina is possibly the prettiest place I've ever been to."

Thatch opened the door to the Mexican supermarket and grinned at me. "I still share an apartment with my ex-husband in Soho. New York is awesome, but every time I come home to Asheville, my heart lifts."

That was the first nice thing he'd said to me since we'd met, though it wasn't really about me. "Well, I'm grateful to have moved here. The city was too hectic, and now all I want is peace."

"Sam, would you kindly grab us a few dozen corn tortillas?" Thatch asked, and he and his sister wandered off.

Sam had apparently been here before, and walked us over to an aisle filled with tortillas and pastries. "I didn't know Mexican cuisine included this kind of stuff." I pointed at a box of shiny brown pastries shaped like curlicues.

"Those are wonderful." Sam snatched the box up. "They're called Orejas. Hey, we forgot to grab a basket. Would you mind getting one for us? We're going to need it."

"Sure." I grinned, then patted him on the ass. Sam turned pink, and my cock twitched. "Be right back."

I walked toward the front of the store, but halfway there I would've sworn I heard my name. I stopped to listen.

"What is Sam doing with Cary in the first place?" Thatch's voice carried over from the next aisle. "He's too old for him."

"Sweetie, if I knew, I'd tell you." Celia Mae replied. "How old was Sam when you and Brian divorced again?"

"Nineteen." Thatch sighed.

"Sam was old enough to know Brian wasn't walking out on him, so I doubt he's looking for a father substitute."

"Why does everyone assume Brian walked out on me?" Thatch grumbled. "Like, do you really believe that he's the only one who wanted out? Though I must admit he's fucked anything that moves since then."

"I was there, big brother. Sorry, that just came out the wrong way." Celia Mae placated him, and I suddenly remembered I was supposed to be fetching a basket. I raced to the front of the store, grabbed one, and went in search of Sam. He wasn't on the aisle where I'd left him, so I headed toward the rear of the store. I found him with Thatch and Celia at what appeared to be a deli counter.

"Hola quisiera una docena de tamales, una libra de machaca y un tarro de mole por favor." Thatch said to the young woman behind the counter.

"That was impressive," I whispered in Sam's ear. "What did he say?"

"He asked for tamales, mole sauce, and machaca's, which is a dried beef." Sam took the basket I was holding and dumped the tortillas and pastries in it. "When my dad got divorced, he started taking Spanish lessons. He's a firm believer in keeping busy and not living in the past. He's almost fluent now."

"Sam, ¿hay algo que quieras?" Thatch asked his son.

"Tomemos flan de postre, papá." Sam replied, and winked at me.

"That was pretty good, too." I grinned at him.

"I am fluent. Spent my sophomore year studying in Mexico City." He said. "Be right back."

Sam walked down the aisle, and I couldn't help but admire his firm, round ass.

"Your eyes are going to fall out, cowboy." Celia Mae rolled her eyes at me, and I felt blood racing up my neck. Then a dude about Sam's age walked past us, wearing a tight red t-shirt, a pair of gray sweatpants, and obviously no underwear. I couldn't tear my eyes off of him.

"Bless your heart, Cary. You're just a raging horn dog." Celia Mae shook her head back and forth.

"Gracias, Mr. Fuller." The woman behind the counter handed Thatch his order. "See you later."

His back was to me, and when he turned around he accidentally, I think, ran over my foot with the grocery cart.

"I'm sorry Cary." Thatch muttered.

"No, it was my fault for standing too close to you." I grinned at him, and he stared at me for a moment.

"So Cary, what do you do for a living?"

"Well, I dabble in a lot of things." I replied and realized Sam was back by my side.

"He used to be in publishing, Dad." Sam piped up.

At that moment I realized exactly who Thatch was, and this was probably a topic best left alone.

"Oh? Would I know the publishing house?" Thatch eyed me.

I sighed. "Cadmus. But after my parents passed away, I sold it to S&S."

"Cadmus! I was published there until... why the hell did you have to sell it?" Thatch's shoulders stiffened. "They were my first publisher, and I would've stayed with them." His fingers tightened on the cart, his knuckles turning white.

"I sold it because I'm not interested in publishing. It was my parents' baby. Now I'm a venture capitalist." I said, hoping he would drop the subject. After I'd sold my interest in Cadmus, I'd gotten quite a lot of blowback from authors who'd been signed to the house. "Mostly, I invest in music streaming and pharmaceutical companies. I'm also thinking about opening an art gallery in Raleigh, but that's for fun."

"Bless your fucking heart, Cary. I thought I recognized your name. Because of you, I lost a considerable amount of money when you sold out." Thatch swung the cart around, barely missing my knee, and stormed toward the front of the store. Celia Mae gave me a withering stare, then headed after her brother.

"Sorry about Dad." Sam squeezed my arm. "He was devastated when his contract was sold to Simon & Schuster."

"I should've left when your father tried to have me arrested."

CHAPTER 4

THATCH

"Would you fetch me the mortar and pestle, Celia Mae." I slid the chopped cilantro into a bowl with the onions. "It's in the cabinet next to the stove."

"You should try joining the twenty-first century big brother and use a food processor." She said, and I could tell she was deliberately provoking me.

"A food processor ruins salsa. It would come out with the texture of soup, and good salsa takes a little elbow grease to make it taste great." I muttered. Moments later, she placed the mortar and pestle next to me. The other reason I wanted it was to relieve some tension. Nothing like hand grinding spices to work off a little steam.

"Dad, how's your novel coming?" Sam asked as he walked into the kitchen. Before I could answer, he swiped a roma tomato out of the small pile in front of me and bit into it like an apple.

I tore off a paper towel and handed it to him, since tomato juice was running down his chin. He loved tomatoes, and had eaten them like this his whole life. "It's, well, frustrating. The characters are chewing me up and spitting me out, over and over again."

"What's the story about?" Celia Mae asked, which surprised me. We rarely ever discussed work. All I knew about her job was she was an administrator at Duke University Hospital in Durham. Celia Mae knew about my work, but when we were together, we mostly gossiped about family and friends.

I opened my mouth to answer right as Cary strolled into the kitchen like he owned the place.

"Um, well, remember my novel Southern Discomfort?" I stammered out.

"Who can forget." Cary grinned, then sat on a stool next to Sam. "You won the Booker Prize for it. My father loved the book, told me all about it."

"You, of all people, shouldn't discuss my publishing career." I bitched, then tossed a handful of garlic cloves into the black granite mortar and began grinding them. Sam cleared his throat and stood.

"For God's sake, Dad. It doesn't matter what Cary says, you find some way to be an asshole. He just complimented you."

I froze, feeling a lump in the back of my throat. Sam was right.

"Cary, forgive me." I resumed grinding the garlic. "The sale of Cadmus Publishing is a sensitive topic for me."

"I understand, Thatch. But indulge me just for a moment." Cary said, so I stopped what I was doing and focused on him. "Let me ask you a question. What did you do for a living before becoming the famous writer you are today?"

"I had a lot of jobs. The last one was," I hummed for a moment, trying to remember. "I worked for a locksmith company as a dispatcher. Damn, when Cadmus signed me for my first book, I quit on the spot. Hated that job."

"I can totally relate, because I hated working in publishing." Cary sighed. "I'm not a writer, an editor, or a marketing specialist. I only owned Cadmus because my Dad left it to me in his will. Honestly, I hated working there. So, I got rid of it."

"Well, that's not the same..."

"Yes it is, Thatch." Celia Mae crossed her arms over her chest. "And it's not like Cary even knew who you were, or did it deliberately."

"I knew who he was, actually." Cary grinned. "But we'd never met. You were one of a handful of authors who kept Cadmus in the black. You might not believe this, but I did you a favor by selling the company."

"Right." I muttered, then poured the cilantro and onions into the mortar and resumed grinding.

"Seriously. I didn't know much about the business, and it was only an income stream for me. You and your books were numbers on a spreadsheet. I don't know who publishes you now, but I can guarantee they care more about your work than I ever did. Having a publishing house who cares about books is better for your work in the long run instead of being with a jerk like me who didn't give a rat's ass." Cary sighed.

"He's got a point, Dad." Sam said, then tried to snatch another tomato away, but I slapped his hand.

"Stop that." I muttered, unsure if I was addressing my son or the strange man he was dating who had spoken the truth.

———

"This meal was exceptional." Cary said, pushing his plate to the side. "There's nothing like real, authentic Mexican food."

"Thanks," I said, forcing myself to smile at him.

"Dad, you never said what your latest book is about." Sam

placed two more tamales on his plate and began removing the husks. He still had the appetite of a teenager.

"It's kind of a continuation of the book Southern Discomfort, but I'm at a bit of a loss about the direction it's heading in. The main character is a divorced man. He's also a writer who tends to be a little self-centered, and high-strung." I drained the rest of my beer and grabbed another one from the ice bucket in the center of the table. "He's controlling, and some would say he is a neurotic know-it-all."

Everyone stared at me, all eyebrows raised toward the ceiling.

"His name is Michael, and he's also a fun guy to be around. I want it to be a comedy, but I'm struggling to make it funny." I sighed.

"Bless your heart, big brother, but you're not exactly known for your sense of humor." Celia Mae stood up, grabbed her empty plate, and walked over to the sink.

"That's not true." I mumbled. "I'm funny."

When Celia Mae sat down again, she turned to Sam. "How did the two of you meet?" She nodded in Cary's direction, who blushed. Swear to God if he says they met on one of those sleazy dating apps, we'll have words.

"Legends." Sam grinned. "You know, the gay nightclub in Raleigh. Me and a couple of buddies from school go every weekend. Cary was there, and we hit it off."

"Have you ever been married, or in a long-term relationship, Cary?" I asked.

"Can't say that I have." He replied, lifting his chin.

"Hmm, I wonder why that is?" Celia Mae snagged a beer out of the bucket.

"Not everyone is the marrying kind, I guess." Cary grinned, but I detected a flinty edge to his voice.

"Dad always taught me to be well-prepared for anything, so

after I met Cary, I did some digging online." Sam whipped out his phone. "He has dated many people, and some of them are famous. Look," Sam handed the phone to Celia Mae.

"You dated Sean Hayes?" Her mouth dropped open.

"Briefly. He was still working on..."

"Will & Grace!" I blurted, then felt embarrassed. But I couldn't help it. That had been my favorite show back in the day.

A toothy smile split Cary's face. "Guys your age always get excited when they hear about me and Sean. He was still keeping his sexuality secret back then, and I'm just not a relationship type of guy. Nothing serious came of it."

Guys my age? Heat raced through me.

"You know what I mean, Thatch." Cary muttered. My annoyance must have shown. "It's not a bad thing to say. I mean, it's just the truth."

"No, I'm sure it was a compliment." I murmured, wishing this weekend would end now.

"If you good people don't mind, I'm going upstairs. I'm suddenly feeling exhausted." Cary got up from his seat. Celia Mae opened her mouth, but I glared at her, so she shut it. "Dinner was exceptional."

The moment we heard his feet on the stairs I turned to Sam. "Why are you dating this asshole?" I whispered. "He's rude, and you know it will never lead to anything serious."

"He's fun." Sam replied.

"What? He's fun?" I threw my hands in the air. "Cary isn't fun, he's just...wrong."

"Wrong can be a lot of fun, Dad."

"Not this fucking wrong." I snapped, and Celia Mae reached over and patted my hand.

"Why don't we not analyze Cary behind his back? Honestly, he's a blast to be around. I've never met someone with a past like his. Dating celebrities, driving a freaking Rolls Royce. Hell, he's a brilliant businessman who has bought and sold multiple companies."

"Who sold my contract to the highest bidder just because he didn't like the job." I got to my feet. "He can't commit to anything. That's why he's..."

"I'm out of here." Sam stood up. "Cary has only said nice things about the two of you, and all you've done is make us both feel unwelcome. We're leaving first thing in the morning, Dad. I'd like to say this has been fun, but I'd be lying."

"Why not leave now? Are the headlights broken on his Rolls Royce?" I regretted the words as soon as they left my lips.

"Dad... screw this." Sam ran out of the kitchen and up the stairs.

"Sam's lying. There's no chance in hell Cary said nice things about us." Celia Mae steepled her fingers under her chin. "We fucked this up, big-time."

"I just, I just, fuck!" I slammed the table with the palm of my hand. "If only he could understand..."

"Dad!!!"

"Was that Sam screaming?" I jumped to my feet. "Sam?" I yelled out. "Is everything okay?"

"Dad!!! Help!!!

CHAPTER 5
THATCH

I raced up the stairs with Celia Mae hot on my heels. Sam's door was wide open, and when I ran into the room, the first thing I noticed was Cary spread-eagled on the bed with his shirt off. A sheen of sweat covered his skin, and he was clutching his chest. Sam stood on the far side of the room, almost as if he were afraid of touching Cary.

"When I walked in he... he was like that." Sam pointed at Cary. "What's happening, Dad?"

"I'll be fine. It was probably something I ate, you know, it was a little spicy." Cary wheezed.

"Cary, are you having chest pains?" Celia Mae pulled her phone out of her sweater pocket.

"It feels like something is pressing down on my chest, like a vise grip is trying to flatten me." Cary inhaled sharply, then rasped, "It's probably nothing."

"I'm calling 911." Celia Mae punched the number into her phone. "You might think this is nothing, but I think you're having a heart attack." She stepped out into the hallway, and moments later was describing Cary's symptoms to a dispatcher.

"Oh, my God, I think I'm passing out." Cary mumbled, and his face lost all color.

"What do we do?!" Sam yelled, tears coursing down his cheeks. "Dad, give him mouth to mouth, or…"

"No, not for a heart attack." My brain was spinning, trying to recall a first aid course me and Brian had taken before adopting Sam. "Damn it, I can't remember what to do!"

I crossed the room and got on the bed, straddling Cary's waist. "Keep your mouth open, Cary," I said, and noticed his eyes were shut. "Fuck," I muttered, then opened his lips with my fingers. "He's unconscious!" I yelled, hoping Celia Mae relayed the info to emergency services.

"Ambulance should be here any minute. Thank God the volunteer rescue squad is close by. I have to run downstairs and open the gate from the control panel. I'll meet them and bring them upstairs." Celia Mae glanced over to Sam. "Come with me, Sam. You'll only get in the way."

Sam ran out of the room and down the stairs, following my sister.

"I'm sorry I was such a dick earlier, but you are a little hard to take sometimes, Cary." His lips suddenly went from purple to blue, and he started gasping for air.

"Shit." I groaned.

Cary's eyes fluttered open. They were bloodshot, and little beads of sweat from his forehead were snaking into his eyes.

"I hope I'm doing the right thing." I bent over to cover his mouth with mine, and his eyes widened. If he could've recoiled, I could guarantee he would have. "Cary, I'm not enjoying this." I bit off the words, then covered his mouth and breathed air down his throat twice.

"Please God, don't let this man die." I muttered, then heard the sound of the ambulance wailing as it raced up the driveway. "You're going to live, Cary, I promise."

"Dad, I don't know anything about Cary's family, or even if he has one. What do we do if he, well, you know?" Tears streamed from my son's eyes. "We've only gone out a few times, like we've known each other for barely two weeks."

"Oh, kiddo, Cary's going to be just fine." I said, patting him on the knee. We were in a waiting room adjacent to the Emergency unit. The hard plastic seats were killing my back.

"People like Cary don't die." Celia Mae murmured. "They enjoy being assholes too much to stop."

"Celia Mae, swear to God you're going to hell." I shook my head, and I heard Sam stifle a sob.

"This is a freaking nightmare. I'm dating a guy so old he takes pills to get it up." Sam choked out. "What the hell is wrong with me?"

"For God's sake, Sam, you're dating a man old enough to have a heart attack! Just let that sink in." I grumbled.

"Thank God you two weren't, you know, messing around. Can you imagine someone having a heart attack while they're inside you?" Celia Mae shuddered, and I did too. "That would scar you for life."

An older nurse at the nursing station across from us cleared her throat. Apparently, our voices had carried.

"I need to rethink my relationship with Cary," Sam moaned. "I'm too young to be a widower."

"You should've thought about that before going on a single date with him." I stood up and paced in front of them. "Why do guys my age feel compelled to go out with dudes half their age? I would hate that. Like, what on earth do you talk about?"

"If I'm guessing right, I bet there wasn't much conversation going on between the two of you, right, Sam?" Celia Mae patted him on the knee.

"You're right, Aunt Celia Mae. Maybe I was blinded by the expensive restaurants and the way he name-dropped celebrities." Sam said, wiping his eyes with the back of his hand. "Older men have always attracted me, but after this, no more."

A tall man in green scrubs strolled over. "Are you the people who called an ambulance for Mr. Lancaster?"

Sam leapt to his feet. "Yes."

"We're treating your father now." He told Sam, who winced. "It will be awhile before we know anything else." The man turned to walk away, but I stopped him with a question.

"Is Cary going to be okay?"

CHAPTER 6

CARY

"Why are you strapping me to the..." I begin, and a plastic mask is placed over my mouth. Suddenly, I could breathe, and I gulped the air in. I'd never been in an ambulance before, and didn't know what the hell was going on. Machines with bright lights lined the walls, and some were even hanging from the roof.

"Five minutes to arrival." I heard a woman's voice squawk from the radio in the front. The driver must have notified the hospital we were almost there, then a man's voice began relaying my symptoms. What he said terrified me

"Patient displayed symptoms of a heart attack, including difficulty breathing, and chest pains. When we placed him on the stretcher, he coughed and blood was present. Now we are..." The sound of his voice faded as a wave of dizziness roared through me. My eyes clamped shut, then I heard doors opening.

"Get him inside, NOW!" A man's voice yelled. I wanted to see what was happening, but I couldn't open my eyes. At that moment, it felt like someone had reached into my chest and squeezed my heart between two fists. Damn it, I wasn't ready to die.

"You're not dying." A voice in my head whispered. I felt a sharp pain in my arm, then the world faded away.

———

"Mr. Lancaster." A woman's voice rang in my ear. "Mr. Lancaster."

My eyes fluttered open. "Are you feeling pain right now?" A woman in surgical scrubs asked. I nodded the best I could with the tubes covering my lower face.

"He's been experiencing chest pain for almost half an hour. He told us he'd felt nauseous and had difficulty breathing. Blood pressure is 170 over 90, pulse is 106. Mr. Lan..." The nurse began, but was interrupted by the doctor.

"He needs an EKG now. My name is Dr. Creighton." The woman said. I heard a creaking sound and saw a machine being rolled next to the bed. Dr. Creighton and the nurse attached me to it with a bunch of cords.

"My chest feels so tight." I muttered, and it felt like a haze had settled over my vision.

"Show me where the pain is." The doctor instructed, and I laid my fist on the right side of my chest. "What were you doing before the onset of symptoms?"

I licked my lips, wondering if I should tell them about the Cialis I'd taken right before dinner. Normally I didn't take boner pills, but Sam's family stressed me out, and I wanted insurance that I could perform. "I had just finished dinner, Mexican food. Then the guy I'm dating came into the room and I was about to kiss him when the pain started."

"So you weren't having intercourse?"

"No, no, hadn't gotten to that stage yet." I replied with a sigh.

"Doctor, I don't think this is a heart attack." The nurse said. "Look at the screen."

Silence hung in the air for a moment, and I felt my pulse ramping up even more.

"Mr. Lancaster, the EKG shows a blocked artery in your lung, which is stressing your heart and making it hard to breathe. Did you take Viagra earlier?" Dr. Creighton asked.

"No," I replied, and she raised an eyebrow.

"The reason I'm asking is there is a rare reaction to that class of medications. I'm suspecting you are experiencing a pulmonary embolism which might be fatal. Now, tell me the truth. Did you take Viagra earlier today?"

"Cialis," I mumbled.

"Same class of drug. Nurse, start him on 3000 units of heparin, and begin aspirin therapy to thin his blood. Mr. Lancaster, what other medications are you taking?" The doctor had a tablet and began typing on it.

"Um, Crestor, and I take Ativan occasionally when I'm feeling anxious." I said, then winced as the nurse inserted the IV.

"Mr. Lancaster, I'm fairly certain that this treatment will work. The medications we're giving you will dissolve the clot in your lung. That's why it's difficult to breathe, and it's putting strain on your heart. We'll talk later about the clot, since it most likely started in your leg then traveled to your lung. Or, the Cialis caused it, we don't know for sure." She tapped on the tablet, then handed it to another nurse I hadn't noticed was there.

"So, Doctor, am I going to live?" I asked, my voice trembling.

"Yes, Mr. Lancaster, you're going to see many more sunrises.

After the blood thinners have a chance to work, we'll have you meet with a nutritionist, since I suspect your diet might be a contributing factor. Do you have any more questions?"

"Is sex off the table forever?" I asked, because now I was terrified of ever taking a boner pill again.

Though her face was covered by a surgical mask, I could see her green eyes crinkle, and suspected she was grinning.

"Let's get you on your feet first, then we'll discuss what you must do to stay healthy in the future. And, a healthier you means you probably won't need to use Cialis or Viagra." Dr. Creighton patted me on the arm, then walked out of the room.

———

When my eyes popped open next, the room was dark, except for the lights from the surrounding machines. I yawned, and my hand automatically went to cover my mouth.

"No IV?" I wondered aloud, then held my arm out in front of me. Maybe this is all a dream. Yeah, it's just a nightmare, though I feel like a tank has run me over.

I pushed the sheets down past my knees, swung my legs over the side of the bed, and gingerly got to my feet. My ears felt blocked, and I shook my head a few times. I sat back down, clutching the mattress.

"Jesus Christ," I breathed. Vertigo, probably. I pushed myself back upright, then slowly I crossed the room to the open door.

The hallway was dimly lit, though I spied a brighter light a few yards away where a blurry figure sat behind a desk. "Not going in that direction." I mumbled, then walked in the opposite way. Double doors were at the end of the hall, and when I got there, I pushed them open.

"Oh my God, it's Cary." I heard Sam's voice and spun around trying to find him.

"Oh, oh, his gown is open in the back!" That was Celia Mae's voicel. I felt like I was drunk, or stoned, which I hadn't been in years. Reaching around me with one hand, I realized she was right, and I'd just flashed everyone.

"Cary, over here!" Sam called out, but everyone's face was a blur. One of the blobs stood and walked toward me, then Sam came into focus.

"I wanna go home. Call my assistant to come get me." I mumbled, then the room began to spin, and my knees buckled.

"Oh my stars," I heard Celia Mae's voice again, and I tried to see where she was, but everything was so fucking blurry. "Whoop! Cary showed his ass again."

"For God's sake, Celia Mae, behave." I heard a man's voice, and realized with dismay it had to be Thatch, the guy who hated me.

"Why do you hate me so much?" I muttered, then his face was next to his son's.

"Sam, go find a nurse. We need to get Cary back to his room." He wrapped his arm around my waist, which shocked me.

"Why are you touching me?" I could hear my voice slurring.

"Sam, go." Thatch ordered. "I've got him. He won't fall."

Suddenly it was just me and Thatch staring into each other's eyes. "You wanna know something?"

"I'm afraid to ask." Thatch said, his arm tightening around my waist.

"You're really good looking for an old dude." I said, then the doors opened behind us and I felt my knees shake.

"I've got him." Thatch said, and a young guy with shoulder-length brown hair and glasses was there in surgical scrubs.

"I'm so sorry, he must have slipped out… hey, aren't you Thatcher Atticus Fuller, the writer?" He asked.

"Yes, but you should…"

"I'm a huge fan of your work. We just read a book of yours in our book club, and…" The man began, but Thatch cut him off.

"Thank you, but you need to take care of Cary now." Thatch eyed the man.

"Are you famous or something?" I mumbled, then the nurse placed his hand on my shoulder and pressed down.

"Oh shit, I'm falling!" I called out, then I was sitting upright in a wheelchair while the room spun around me. "I'm so dizzy."

"Let's get you back to your room, sir. Then you can go back to sleep." The nurse turned the chair toward the double doors and pushed me forward. As we exited the waiting room, I heard Celia Mae's voice ring out.

"You got to admit that's one helluv an ass for a man that age."

CHAPTER 7
THATCH

"What the hell is wrong with these people?" I fumed. "They're letting patients just wander the hallways while whacked out on drugs?"

"Hell, that nurse was positively fan girling you." Celia Mae noted. "He was easy on the eye, if you know what I mean." She picked up a tattered magazine, then tossed it back on the side table. "Why are we still here?"

"We can't just leave Cary all alone in a hospital." Sam said, and I noticed dark circles stretching halfway down his cheeks. Glancing at my watch, I saw it was past two in the morning.

"Sam's right. We can't dump him off at the hospital and leave without knowing what's going on with him." I sighed, then pushed myself off the hard plastic seat. "I'll be back as soon as I can find out what's ..."

"Are you the people who brought in Cary Lancaster?" A woman with curly blonde hair in a ponytail said as she strolled into the waiting room. Accompanying her was the nurse who'd taken Cary back to his room.

"Yes," Sam said, getting to his feet. Celia Mae yawned and remained seated.

"I'm Dr. Creighton, and this is Joey Davies, the nurse looking after him. Sorry it's taken us a while to get back to you, but it's been a crazy night in the ER." She smiled, and the nurse stared at his feet.

"This is my son, Sam," I gestured toward him. "Celia Mae is my sister, and I'm Thatch Fuller. Cary is a…" I didn't quite know what to call him. "… a friend of the family."

Celia Mae coughed.

"Mr. Lancaster didn't have a heart attack." The doctor stated.

"Oh, thank God." Sam exclaimed.

"Since you aren't his immediate family, I can't go into much detail." Dr. Creighton said, then turned to the nurse. "Can I see his file?"

The nurse handed her a tablet, and she pecked at it for a moment. "Mr. Lancaster had a blood clot in his lung, which we successfully dissolved, but he isn't out of the woods just yet. Does he have family nearby?"

"No, I think he was an only child, and both his parents are dead." Sam answered, and for the first time, I felt sorry for him. The man might be a wealthy asshole, but it seemed to me he had little in the way of family or friends.

Dr. Creighton's lips pressed together, and she typed something on the tablet. "Again, I can't go into specifics, but Mr. Lancaster is on the mend. His last EKG reading came out normal, but at his age, he will need a little extra time to heal." She handed the tablet back to the nurse. "I'll let Nurse Davies handle things from here."

He took the tablet and opened his mouth to speak, but Dr. Creighton hurried away. His discomfort was obvious.

"Do you know when he will be released?" Sam asked.

"I can't say for sure, but probably within forty-eight hours." He murmured, then turned to me. "Mr. Fuller, I apologize for my behavior earlier. I was a little starstruck when I realized who you were, but that's no excuse for being unprofessional."

"Don't worry," Sam piped up. "It happens to Dad all the time."

"Well, not that often." I murmured. "God, this entire experience was so intense." I sat down next to Celia Mae, who patted me on the leg.

"We never know when the unexpected will happen." Nurse Davies said, and I'd swear he winked at me. "Dr. Creighton gave Mr. Lancaster something to help him sleep, so you guys might want to consider going home and getting some rest, too. I have to get back to work. It was a pleasure to meet you, Mr. Fuller, and your family."

As soon as the nurse exited the waiting room, Celia Mae turned to Sam. "That's the man you should go for. He's still a little older than you, but not by multiple decades. He has a great job, and to top it off, he likes to read books. That's always how you spot a good guy. Books." She pushed herself to her feet, then held out her hand to pull me up.

"Matchmaking in the ER." I grabbed her hand and got to my feet. "I should write a book about it."

"Aunt Celia Mae, that man is not interested in me. His eyes were glued to Dad." Sam patted me on the shoulder, and we all strolled toward the exit.

"Kiddo, Nurse Davies has to be at least twenty years younger than me." I chuckled. "I prefer men closer to my age."

"Well, stud, where the hell are they?" Celia Mae grinned. "And who says you can't have a fling with a younger man? If Cary can do it, why not you?"

The automatic doors opened, and we strolled out of the hospital. A full moon was attempting to break through the clouds, and crickets were singing. "And look what happened to him."

"Dad, the dude likes you. It was obvious to both of us. He seems like a decent guy, and he's not bad looking." Sam said as we all got into my car.

"He doesn't like me. That guy, Joey, likes my books. There's a huge difference, and half the time a writer meets a fan, they have bizarre notions about what we're like in private. They think we live our lives with our heads in the clouds, constantly dreaming up fresh stories. There's so much more to us." I switched on the ignition and backed the car out of the parking space.

"But, Dad, you just described yourself to a T." Sam yawned.

"This is insane. I'd never..."

"You are going to end up a lonely old man if you don't take a chance every once in a while." Celia Mae interrupted. "You haven't gone out with anyone since the divorce. It's like you aren't even trying."

"Maybe I don't want to," I lied. "I spent over twenty years with Brian, and now I'm enjoying a little alone time."

"You guys divorced five years ago. My other dad has dated lots of guys since then." Sam said.

"That's because Brian is a gentleman of easy virtue," Celia Mae drawled. "Just can't keep it in his pants."

"Shut up, Aunt Celia Mae." Sam's words slurred, and I could tell he was about to pass out. "Dad didn't wallow after the divorce. He got on with his life."

I sighed, then turned the car toward home. "Maybe I should too."

———

On Saturday, Dr. Creighton told us she was releasing Cary the next day. Celia Mae and I stayed out of Cary's room, but Sam was allowed to visit him. He stayed with him for about an hour, then we all returned to my house. Sam mostly stayed in his bedroom, recovering from the shock. I never asked him what he said to Cary while they were alone, but I had a feeling he was figuring out a way to break things off with him, without hurting his feelings too much.

Sunday morning, the three of us headed back to the hospital to say our goodbyes. Sam had Cary's bag that he'd left at the house and told us Cary's assistant was driving in from Raleigh to collect him.

When we arrived in the waiting room, we noticed a tall skinny woman dressed head-to-toe in Gucci talking to the nurses at the desk.

"... no, I promise Cary will take it easy for the next few weeks." She tossed her stick-straight black hair back. "If we need to, I'll get a private nurse to look after him."

"Are you Cary's assistant?" Sam asked her. She spun around and grinned, and I noticed a fleck of red lipstick staining her front tooth.

"You must be Sam." She held her hand out for him to shake. "I'm Jenny Sakura, Cary's personal assistant. He's only said wonderful things about you and your family."

Sam glanced down at his feet, and at that moment, I knew he was breaking things off with Cary.

"Here I am!" Cary called out. Joey Davies pushed him into the lobby in a wheelchair with Dr. Creighton by his side. He tried to stand up, but Joey placed a hand on his shoulder to hold him down.

"Not until we are outside the hospital, Mr. Lancaster." Joey grinned, and again, I'd swear that he winked at me. Celia Mae elbowed me in the side and cleared her throat.

"Before we leave, I have something to give you, Dr. Creighton." Cary nodded at his assistant, who opened her Gucci bag and pulled out a flat baby-blue velvet box. "You've taken excellent care of me, and I appreciate it."

Dr. Creighton eyed the gift. "This is my job, and I don't expect presents."

"Well, go on, open it." Cary smiled. "The best part of giving a gift is seeing how happy it makes someone."

Moments later, she lifted the lid and gasped. "You, you can't be serious. These are black pearls. They must be worth a fortune."

"Worth every penny," Cary grinned up at her. "Without you, I'd be pushing up daisies."

"I can't accept this. It's way too generous." She tried to hand the box to Cary's assistant, who refused to take it.

"Dr. Creighton likes the pearls." Cary winked at us. "Let's get out of here, so she can't give it back. Jenny, we have to go to Thatch's home first to get my car. Would you mind following behind us in your car, so I can say goodbye to the Fullers?" She nodded. "Joey, take me to the parking lot."

As we walked through the sliding doors, Dr. Creighton kept trying to give the pearls back to Jenny, who ignored her. Once we were outside, Cary stood up from the wheelchair, wobbling.

"Dr. Creighton, turn around. I'm going to put this necklace on you. Once you feel the delicate pearls against your skin, you'll fall in love with it. Jenny, give me the box." Cary ordered. Jenny took the box from the doctor and handed it to Cary.

"I'm not joking, Mr. Lancaster. This gift is too much." Dr. Creighton crossed her arms across her chest. Jenny squinted at her. Without saying another word, she grabbed the doctor by the shoulders and spun her around so Cary could clasp the necklace around her neck.

He pulled the strand of pearls out of the box, took a step

toward the doctor and with a howl, fell flat on his ass. We all jumped back at the same time.

"Cary!" Sam yelled.

"Oh shit." Celia Mae muttered.

"My God, Mr. Lancaster!" Dr. Creighton spun around. "I knew this was too soon. You can't travel like this. You're not strong enough."

"I'm not going back in there." Cary growled. "You can't make me."

Joey dropped to his knees and began taking Cary's pulse. "Dr. Creighton, besides being a little excited, he's fine." I noticed a pleading look in his eyes, like he wanted to get rid of Cary. If he was a pain in the ass with normal people, he probably made the staff at the hospital insane.

"Sorry, but I can't allow Mr. Lancaster to travel back to Raleigh." Dr. Creighton sighed. "If you can find accommodations here in Asheville, I'll release him."

"Dad." Sam rubbed my shoulder. "Do you think you could…"

"Oh, hell," I groaned. "Sam, you can't be serious."

"Please, let him stay with you, Dad. It's only for a few days. I'd stay too, but I have school tomorrow." Sam's glossy eyes bored into mine. He knew I couldn't say no to him when he looked at me like that.

"Jesus, fine, but just for a few days." I felt pressure building behind my eyes. Sam was leaving with Celia Mae, who had to be in Durham tomorrow for work. I glanced over at Cary's assistant, who was arguing with the doctor and nurse. It was like chaos followed Cary everywhere he went. Would his assistant be staying with me, too?

Celia Mae shook her head. "Bless your heart, Thatch. Hope you and your new roommate have a fabulous time together."

CHAPTER 8
CARY

"I never thought I'd say this, but I'm sick of being in bed," I sighed. Sam was stuffing his overnight bag with clothes for his return trip to Chapel Hill. He'd been solicitous, kind, and a good friend, but he'd avoided making eye contact since we returned to his father's house.

"You need to rest, otherwise you might get sick again." Sam zipped up the bag, then perched on the corner of the bed and patted my leg. "I need to tell you something."

My shoulders slumped since I knew what was coming. "You've decided it's best we remain friends? Of the platonic variety, I'm assuming." I smoothed the orange bedspread down over my lap. Glancing up, I noticed Sam's bright-blue eyes staring at the wall. They were shiny, as if he was about to cry.

"We had a great time together while it lasted, Cary. But, I have too much going on at school. I'm giving my dissertation in two months, and I've barely scratched the surface of my thesis." He said, getting to his feet.

"And what you aren't saying is that I'm too old." I

murmured, and Sam froze. "Hey, maybe this is my come-to-Jesus moment. I haven't been taking care of myself, and maybe it's just the end of the line for me, and dating."

"Knock-knock."

Sam and I turned to the door to behold my assistant, Jenny.

"Thatch thought you might be hungry after being in the hospital, so he made a meal for you." She marched over and set a tray on my lap.

"Is he trying to starve me to death?" I shook my head. A bowl of sliced fruit, a bottle of Italian dressing, and a plate of salad greens stared back at me. I noticed a piece of paper next to the food with Jenny's spidery cursive on it.

Should I cancel your dinner reservation with William Thornton and send flowers instead?

Will was another twink I'd been seeing. Might as well end that now, too. "Jenny, give me a..."

"Sam, you ready to go?" Celia Mae asked from the doorway. Her blonde hair was piled high on her head, and she was holding a Louis Vuitton suitcase.

"Yeah," Sam replied, and trudged up to the head of the bed. I flipped the note over so he wouldn't see it. "I'll call you later this week to check on you." He leaned down, pecked me on the cheek, then turned to Jenny. "Take good care of him."

Once Celia Mae and Sam were gone, I gazed up at Jenny. "When you cancel dinner with Will, tell him I will call him soon." I was going to end things with him, but wasn't going to delegate that task to Jenny. She had enough on her plate since I'd be out of the office.

"Of course." She whipped out her phone and made a note. "By the way, that nurse," she tapped at her phone's screen, "Joey Davies. He's agreed to come here daily to make sure you are recovering properly."

"I am paying him, right?"

"Of course. Now, what is happening with me? Do you need me to stay here with you, or do you want me to return to Raleigh and work out of the office?"

"If you could work out of my office at home instead of the business office, I'd be grateful. You can stay there too, since I'll be here for the next few days. I'd have you remain here, but I don't want to impose on our host. Thatch is already going above and beyond the call of duty. Come up with a few ideas for gifts I can send him after this ordeal is over with." I picked up a fork and speared a wedge of cantaloupe.

"Will do." Jenny smiled and slipped her phone back in her purse, then she sat on the bed next to me. "Are you going to be alright here?"

Jenny was the only employee I considered a friend, and I could depend on her for anything. She'd worked for me for almost ten years. "Yes. Get out of here. If you leave now, you'll make it back to Raleigh before dark."

"Yes, sir." She kissed me on the forehead, got to her feet, and left.

Once she was gone, I grabbed my phone off the nightstand and searched through my contacts. Not that I wanted to text or call anyone.

"All these twinks gotta go." I sighed. "Richard, with your donkey dick and adorable dimples. Haven't seen you since I left New York, so at least I don't have to tell you goodbye." I removed his contact info. "Enrique, fuck, I hate to end it with you, but adios." I removed his info too, then set the phone down and swiped a tear off my cheek.

"Nothing like almost dying to realize you've gotten old." I opened the bottle of salad dressing and drenched the greens with it. It was like walking through a closing door, saying goodbye to both my youth, and to the young men I'd worshiped. All I could see was a future filled with tasteless salads, doctor visits, and lots of me time.

"Do I even like myself enough to continue on? Or should I just buy a retirement home and move into it already?" I said, then stuffed another mouthful of lettuce into my mouth. Hmm, a gay retirement home might make money. I picked up my phone and sent Jenny a text asking her to look into it.

"How are you feeling, Cary?"

I looked up to see Thatch standing in the doorway with his arms crossed over his chest.

"Hey, are you okay?" Thatch crossed the room and stood next to the bed. "Have you been crying?"

I leaned my head against the headboard and shut my eyes. "Maybe."

"It's totally normal. You know, being emotional after what you've been through. I read an article about how near-death experiences trigger some people." Thatch said, and I felt him pat my shoulder.

For the first time, I really noticed his voice. His words had a cadence I wasn't used to, almost like he was reading a book to a small child. That made sense since he was a writer. And his accent. Well, if I kept my eyes shut, I could see a younger version of Thatch. Instead of his wavy salt and pepper hair, I pictured his hair being dark, like Sam's. I realized his son was adopted, but I would lay money on them having the same wavy dark-brown hair.

"You don't have to talk. Sorry if I interrupted…" Thatch began, and I opened my eyes and grinned at him.

"I don't mind," I sighed. "Thanks for feeding me. Actually, thank you for all of this. You didn't have to take me in. Honestly, I'm not used to feeling so helpless."

"What Sam wants, he usually gets." Thatch crossed his arms

over his chest and stared down at me. He had brilliant-blue eyes like his son, except they had little crinkles around them. "I've tried not to spoil him, but it's hard not to. Brian and I knew he was being raised in a different environment than his peers, you know, having two fathers. We gave him everything he wanted, within limits, obviously."

"You raised a wonderful child. It's funny, even though I know he's adopted, Sam resembles you."

"Sam's birth mother is my cousin. She was a teenager when she had him, and didn't feel like she was prepared to do right by Sam." Thatch's eyes wandered around the room, landing on the wooden dresser drawers. "That's a lot of flowers. Who sent them?"

"Jenny. She keeps my home filled with beautiful arrangements, and she decided to do the same here. Best assistant I've ever had." I grinned up at him. "So, does Sam know his birth mother?"

"Oh, yes, they've met." Thatch got to his feet and paced around the room, wiping away imaginary dust from the furniture. "Sharon, that's her name, sees him around the holidays every year. They aren't exactly friends, but they are friendly." Thatch turned and raised an eyebrow in my direction. "You won't be needing those here." He pointed at the nightstand, stomped over, and scooped up my stash of cigars.

"Another pleasure, gone for eternity." I sighed. "No sex, love, or delicious food. Hell, let's just call this the no fun allowed zone." I threw my hands up in the air. "What the hell do people like you do for fun?" I asked Thatch, then regretted it. "I'm sorry. I shouldn't have said it quite the way I did."

Thatch reached down and removed the tray from my lap. "I'm a fun guy." He mumbled, then he beamed at me with a twinkle in his eye. "Have you ever thought that the life you were living wasn't fun? That you were running on a treadmill of denial about reality?"

"What do you mean?"

CHAPTER 9

THATCH

f I had to describe Cary, the first thing that came to mind was the man was a cad, who only lived for sexual excess and debauchery. That was because I was a writer, and I had a bad habit of slotting people into neat little categories. Underneath his veneer of sophistication, I could see a man who was lost, so when he asked me what I meant by his being in denial about reality, I struggled to keep my words kind.

"Do realize I'm going on assumptions here, but from everything you've said, and from what Sam has told me, you spend a lot of time chasing younger men. If I dare guess, it's been like a game to you." I sat on the edge of the bed and smiled at him.

"Well, yes, I used to, though I think I've been permanently benched by the big coach in the sky." Cary pointed up toward the heavens.

"How old are you?" I asked, wondering if he'd tell the truth.

"Forty-nine." Cary's lips pressed together, and his eyes shut.

"Is this your first health scare?"

Cary swallowed, then murmured, "Yes."

"Reality is slapping you upside the head right now. Going

to nightclubs and chasing after men half your age takes up a lot of time and energy. I'm no expert, but I'd say that you're addicted to the chase, almost like an alcoholic craves booze." I watched as my words sank in. Cary was a handsome man, even when he was under the weather. His salt and pepper hair was cut short, and he had the sharpest cheekbones I'd ever seen on a man. The only evidence of illness was the color of his skin, which was still a little too pale.

"I'm not an alcoholic," Cary murmured, his eyes still shut.

"No, I didn't say that. What I meant was that chasing younger men is similar to an addiction. It's something you've spent a lot of time on, and I guarantee that every time you scored with a young guy, you'd feel high. You know, like an adrenaline rush." I stood and strolled over to the door.

"When's the last time you... never mind." Cary mumbled, his eyes now trained on me.

"You know what fun is?" I asked, and Cary said nothing. "It's waking up refreshed everyday, knowing you are healthy enough to get your work done. You also have more time, since you're not wasting days and days on the chase. Plus, drama is kept to a minimum. God, if I had to date a younger version of myself, I'd tear my hair out. Guys in their twenties don't have a clue about how the real world works. But, it's your life, Cary. I hope you make the best of the time you have left."

I was about to walk through the door when Cary's voice stopped me cold.

"But, don't you miss love?"

I turned back toward him and opened my mouth to speak, but nothing came out.

"You do, don't you?" A Mona Lisa smile settled on his face, then I backed out of his room, not admitting to him he was right.

———

Monday morning I entered my sacred space, also known as my office. It was on the third floor, and stretched halfway across the house. The rear wall was one large window with a view of a waterfall coming from the Cullajasa River. It was stunning year round, but more so in the winter. Enormous icicles formed every January, and it always took my breath away just looking at it.

This was where I felt the most peaceful and creative, and nearly all of my books had been written here. This was the one part of the house considered off-limits to everyone, except for twice a year when the cleaning service was allowed inside to clean the windows.

There was a small kitchenette where I kept cokes in a mini-fridge along with snacks. My expectation was to write a chapter per day. Unfortunately, the words I normally considered my friends had abandoned me. I grabbed a coke out of the fridge and settled behind my desk. Then I grabbed a few peanuts out of a crystal bowl and poured them into the coke bottle. When I switched on the desktop computer, my phone pinged.

"Shit," I muttered. It was a message from Brian.

Where are you? Video meeting now

Damn it, I'd forgotten, thanks to the chaos of the weekend. Every Monday, Brian and I would meet for a few minutes to discuss Sam, books, and business.

Moments later Brian's face filled the screen.

"What's wrong?" He asked, taking off his glasses and cleaning them with the front of his shirt.

"What do you mean? Why do you think something's wrong?" I sighed and waited for the inevitable lecture. Brian was invaluable as an agent and as a friend, but he could be very bossy.

"You haven't shown me any pages from your current work in progress. That's not like you." Brian combed his dyed brown hair back with his fingers.

"Well, things have been a little hectic around here. Have you talked with Sam?" I asked.

"No. The little twerp has been avoiding me for the last couple of weeks. Why? Is he in trouble?"

I chuckled, because I knew exactly why Sam had been avoiding him, and he was currently living in Sam's bedroom. "He hasn't told you about his last, um, boyfriend, huh?"

Brain grabbed a pen and scrawled something down, probably a note to call Sam. "Why does he always confide in you and not me?"

"Because, you still treat him like a fifteen-year-old. In case you've forgotten, he's twenty-four and in graduate school. Like, he's an adult now. Stop calling him twerp." I shook my head, knowing what I was saying would go in one ear and out the other, then I noticed a figure in the corner of the screen. It was a man about Sam's age wearing only a towel. "Christ." I muttered.

"Okay, so what's going on with Sam. And then I need you to promise me you'll have pages to show your editor by the end of next week. Sales were a little slow on your last release, and they're getting worried." The man in the towel glanced up, realized he was on the screen and hurried out of the room. I didn't think Brian had noticed.

"Well, he thought I was going to the beach house for the weekend, and brought a guy here. I didn't know, of course. We strolled into the kitchen to find a man in his underwear raiding the fridge. Celia Mae nearly attacked him with a butcher knife."

Brian threw back his head and laughed. "What's the big deal? Sam's had boyfriends before. Why didn't he talk to me about him?"

I took a swig of my coke and burped. "Excuse me. Um, well, this man is a little older than..." My words died in my throat, remembering the young man I'd just seen in a towel behind Brian.

"How much older?"

"He's forty-nine, and he nearly died in Sam's bed last Friday."

Brian's mouth dropped open.

"So, we spent most of the weekend at the hospital. Now he's in Sam's bedroom recuperating. He had a pulmonary embolism, but at first we thought it was a heart attack." My eyes shut for a moment, and when I opened them, Brian's face was twisted in a scowl.

"What the hell is Sam thinking? That guy is twice his age. I hope you read him the riot act. Damn it, he's going to hear it from me about this. He's a smart kid, but this is possibly the stupidest thing I've ever..."

"As stupid as the twink in the towel running around behind you?" I pushed my chair back an inch, and put my feet up on the desk. Brian swiveled his head around, and when he looked back at me his face was decidedly purple. "You are such a hypocrite."

Brian reached forward, and the screen went black.

"Bless your heart, Brian, your porch light is on, but no one's home." I laughed, and a sense of relief washed through me. No more video calls from him for at least a month.

When Brian and I met, it had been love at first sight, at least for me. Couldn't read his mind, but judging by the first few years we were together he felt the same. By the time Sam was in middle school we were hitting the skids.

The love was still there, and a calmer version of that love still existed for me, but the passion we'd once shared had vanished. I remembered the therapist I was seeing at the time comforting me, even making me laugh about it.

"Ya'll are experiencing the gay version of what's known as lesbian bed death." She'd cracked. Since she was a lesbian, I figured she knew what she was talking about. "Night after night, holding hands, praying for a single erotic urge to pass between you, but alas, once bed death creeps in, the end is usually near."

Huh. Maybe I needed to schedule an appointment with her, because it looked like the only men who wanted me were much younger, and I was attracted to men my age. Perhaps I needed to come to grips with growing old alone?

Once you passed the forty-year mark, men lost interest in you, which was a shame. Cary was an exceptionally attractive man, well, when his mouth was shut. Maybe if he... nah. Cary was a lost cause. Hopefully he'd make peace with himself, and learn to accept the inevitable.

"Keeping up with kids is hard work, and once you reach a certain age it's just not worth it." I shook my head, then pulled my phone out and searched through my contacts. "There you are."

I placed the call, and moments later a soothing male voice answered the phone.

"Blue Ridge Pride Behavioral Associates. How may I assist you?"

CHAPTER 10

CARY

Sam's bedroom was obviously decorated for a teenage boy, albeit a wealthy kid's room. It was spacious, with shiny hardwood floors and a giant window facing a lush, green, forest. The first three feet of the walls were painted dark brown, then it was white all the way up to the ceiling. On the nightstand was a framed photo of Sam with Thatch.

"What an interesting life you've had, kiddo." I murmured, then shut my eyes and replayed the last encounter with my host.

Thatch seemed to be under the impression that all I did was chase twinks, that there was nothing more to me than that. Maybe one day we'd sit down and have a drink together, and I'd tell him about myself. How I'd inherited a small sum from my grandparents when I was fresh out of high school and started the first of many successful businesses. My problem was my inability to stay focused for long periods of time.

Whenever a business started turning a profit, I'd lose interest. That was when I'd sell it. Let someone else deal with the dreary day-to-day operations. All I wanted was that feeling of creating something new, then it lost its luster and I'd say adios.

"Kind of like me and men." I sighed. Maybe one of the reasons I preferred younger guys was their freshness, and energy. Until, of course, it no longer felt fresh and energetic. As soon as that happened I'd give them a parting gift, like they did on those tacky game shows. Let them know how I appreciated spending time with them, but it was time to move on. None of them had ever felt slighted, I thought, or at least no one had ever complained to my face.

"Why did I say that to Thatch?" Asking him if he missed love when I'd never felt it before myself? Probably because he made me uncomfortable, and it was my way of protecting myself. Since he discovered me going through his fridge, Thatch had treated me with something approaching disdain. Whatever the reason, Thatch made me feel on edge, which no one ever did.

He was a good-looking man, but guys his age wanted more than a simple fling. They were more demanding and had too much baggage to make me want to pursue them. Hell, I didn't even have friends his age. We had little in common beyond an excess of birthdays, and who liked to dwell on those?

Thatch had been prickly, but he'd also been incredibly kind by letting me stay here. It would probably have been better if I'd just booked a hotel room nearby and hired a private nurse to look after me. But, Sam had insisted, and now I was living under the watchful eye of my host. Perhaps I should try to get to know him better?

———

"Damn it."

My laptop needed recharging, and I had nothing else to

keep me busy. I was sick of watching cat videos anyway. For some reason I found them soothing, hypnotic almost. When they proved boring I'd switch over to videos starring huskies. I could have watched videos on my phone, but I hated the tiny screen.

"What's that smell?" I sniffed the air and my stomach growled. The rabbit food I'd been fed hadn't filled me, and now I could smell actual food being cooked down in the kitchen. My mouth watered, and instead of sitting here with nothing to do but starve, I decided to risk the stairs and fill my stomach. I kicked the sheets off and swung my feet to the floor. Then I braced the mattress with both my hands and pushed myself up.

"Oh shit," I groaned as the room spun around. Praying I didn't fall backward, I forced my feet to move forward. So far all I'd attempted was getting from the bed to the bathroom, and the first few steps were always the hardest. My robe was draped over a chair next to the door, and when I reached it I gripped the back of it to regain my breath. It wasn't like I was in physical pain, it was that everything I did required lots of effort. But, I was so fucking hungry, I'd do anything for a proper meal.

After tying the sash to my robe I slipped my phone into the pocket, then slowly turned to the door and opened it, wincing at the creak it made. It was like being a teenager again, sneaking out of my room in the middle of the night, so I could slip out of the house unnoticed. I'd bought my first fake ID when I was sixteen and loved to hit the gay clubs. Like all kids, I got off on putting one over on my parents. Slipping the maid a few bucks on those nights ensured I wouldn't be caught.

The stairs weren't horribly steep, so I gripped the wooden handrail and prayed I didn't slip on the bright red runner. That's when I heard the sound of a man's voice singing.

"Not bad, Thatch." I panted, then a bolt of dizziness hit me and I sat down on a step to catch my breath. "Jesus, I must be sicker than I thought."

"What the hell are you doing out of bed, Cary?"

"Oh shit." I muttered. At the bottom of the steps Thatch had his hands on his hips and was shaking his head. "I've been caught red-handed."

"I'll bring you dinner. You should be upstairs." Thatch started up the steps and I held my hand up for him to stop.

"I can do this." I wheezed, and forced myself to my feet. "Whatever you're cooking smells amazing."

Thatch stared at me a second, and a moment later he was standing in front of me. "Let's get you back to bed."

"No," I shouted. "Shit, I didn't mean to yell. Look, I have to get out of there for a few minutes. Those four walls are making me crazy. Please, let me just sit in the kitchen with you. Maybe I can help? You know, with dinner?"

"You've never cooked anything before in your life that didn't involve a microwave, right?" Thatch's lips twitched, like he was forcing himself not to smile.

"So? I can learn."

His intense blue eyes bored into mine, then a true smile split his face. "Well then, let's get you to the kitchen. You can snap the beans."

"I have no idea what that entails, but if you just let me sit with you awhile, I'll do whatever you ask." I met his smile with one of my own. Thatch put a hand in front of my face and I grabbed it. A moment later I was swaying on my feet, so he put an arm around me and slowly we trudged down the stairs. He had a strong grip, and I wondered if he worked out.

"You have some fancy-ass pj's on. Where did you get those?" Thatch asked. "Were they a gift from the Queen or something?"

"Jenny got them for me. She does all my shopping, well,

and just about everything else, too." I glanced down at my clothes. My robe was black silk with a white fur collar, and my pajamas were royal purple with gold piping. By now we were at the last step, and once my feet were firmly planted on the floor Thatch let go of me.

"Are you okay to walk by yourself now?"

"Never better," I breathed, then I slowly followed Thatch to the kitchen.

"Here, sit on this stool and let me get the beans." Thatch pointed to the seat, then opened the fridge. He grabbed a large plastic bowl out of it and placed it in front of me.

"So these are green beans," I said. "How do you 'snap' them?"

Thatch grinned and placed a smaller bowl next to the larger one. "It's simple." He snatched a green bean out of the bowl and broke the ends off, dropping them in the smaller bowl. "Notice the satisfying pop it gives when you snap the ends off."

"This might prove to be fun." I smiled, then went to work. "So what were you singing earlier? You have a nice voice."

"I didn't know you could hear me all the way upstairs. That was the late, great, Patsy Cline. My favorite song of hers is called I Fall to Pieces." He proceeded to sing a few bars, and I had to admit it was a little too country for my taste. I preferred dance music. "Why don't we listen to her singing instead of mine. Trust me, I've never met a soul who didn't love her voice."

Thatch stepped out of the kitchen for a moment, then a woman's rich alto came through hidden speakers. Thatch came back and stared at me, with a glimmer in his eye. After she sang the chorus I commented.

"I'm impressed. Excellent vocal technique."

"Patsy nursed me through some rough times with Brian.

Better than whiskey, and not even a whiff of a hangover."
Thatch grinned.

"So what are you cooking besides green beans?"

"I already fried the chicken. Now I'm working on spoon
bread." Thatch reached into the fridge and pulled out a bowl of
eggs.

"What on earth is spoon bread?"

"It's the reason yankees like you fall in love with southern
cooking."

"Country music, southern cooking. You're a good 'ol boy
through and through." I said, then realized I'd snapped the last
bean. "All done with these."

"The novel I'm struggling with is set in the deep south. I'm
trying to put myself in the mood to write it, but it's been difficult." Thatch said while measuring flour into a cup. My phone
buzzed in my pocket, so I pulled it out and grimaced.

Will Thornton, the guy I had Jenny send flowers to. His text
message demanded that I call him right now. "Will you excuse
me for a moment?" I slowly got to my feet and wandered into
the living room.

Maybe Thatch had a point about younger guys, especially
this one. Will was a messy drama queen. When I reached the
sofa I eased myself down and punched Will's number.

"You're breaking up with me, aren't you?" Were the first
words out of his mouth.

"Hi, sweetheart. Sorry I had to cancel our date, but something came up." Will didn't need to know why I couldn't make
it. "Did you like the flowers I sent you?"

"Why did you cancel?" He asked with a trembling voice.
"Have I done something wrong?"

"No, no, no. I just can't make it. I'm stuck in the mountains
due to an unfortunate, um, thingy." I sighed, then noticed
Thatch leaning against the wall a few feet away with his arms

crossed over his chest. "When I return to Raleigh I'll let you know, okay?"

I didn't give Will a chance to reply, and ended the call.

"If you think I'm pleased you've been seeing my son, you're wrong. But, I also don't like hearing you making plans with other guys. Are you cheating on Sam?"

"Thatch, your son broke up with me before he left with your sister." Why the hell was he giving me a hard time? He didn't want me dating Sam.

"Be that as it may, it's very... he did?"

CHAPTER 11

THATCH

"Yes." Cary said, then wandered back to the kitchen and sat at the counter. "And we weren't in a committed, monogamous relationship. Sam knew I was seeing other men, and he could've been too. I'm not concerned about what he was doing when he wasn't with me."

"Well, I guess it's none of my business what types of relationships Sam has, but I never thought of him being into open relationships. Nothing wrong with that, of course." I muttered, then went to the fridge and pulled out the other ingredients for spoon bread. Brian and I had raised Sam in a somewhat traditional family structure. A few months before the divorce, Brian had suggested we open the relationship to spice things up. I'd balked. Having a revolving door to our bedroom with a cast of strange men was a total turnoff.

"Sam told me you were conservative when it came to sex and love. Honestly, I don't believe he wanted us to even meet. He guessed you would disapprove of me, and I would lay money on him being right." Cary eyed me, then threw his hands in the air. "What can I do to help with this spoon bread stuff?"

This revelation about Sam had my brain spinning. I thought he was more like me. While I had numerous friends in non-monogamous relationships, I had never found it appealing. It always seemed too complicated. Instinctively, I preferred being faithful to one man.

"If you insist on helping, I'm going to give you a cooking lesson." I placed all the ingredients in front of Cary, who eyed me suspiciously.

"Are you sure you want me cooking? Because I've never done it before in my life." Cary picked an egg out of the bowl and held it close to his eyes before setting it back.

"Spoon bread is one of the easiest dishes to make, and it tastes out of this world." I said, relieved to be talking about something else. "In front of you are cornmeal, eggs, butter, salt, milk, and baking powder. The first thing we're going to do is boil a cup of water."

Cary started to get up from his seat, but I stopped him. "Don't worry, I'll take care of the water." I poured a cup of water into a saucepan and turned the heat on high. "So, why did you and Sam choose to be in an open relationship?"

Shit. I need to drop the subject.

"Well. I think you are mistaking what Sam and I had with what you and your ex-husband had. Remember, your son and I only dated for two

weeks or so. It wasn't a serious thing." Cary tilted his head to the side, but his gaze never left mine. "Like, remember when you were young and went on actual dates with guys?"

I nodded.

"It's a common practice for people of any sexual orientation to casually date, and often it's with more than one person. I've never been in a committed relationship with anyone, and prefer to play the field."

"Why?" I asked. "I mean, why haven't you ever…?"

"I would love to say something profound or deep, but I've never met a guy I wanted to be exclusive with." Cary's smile spread slowly across his face. "The water is boiling."

"Oh, yes, it is." I turned off the burner, then poured the cornmeal and salt into a large glass bowl and put it in front of Cary. "This is a whisk." I handed it to him. "Start stirring the flour with this, and I'll drizzle the hot water into it. Don't stop stirring until I tell you to."

"Yes, sir." Cary began to stir, and I picked up the pan and began pouring.

"Why do you think you haven't fallen for anyone?" I asked, and a drop of hot water flew up and hit my cheek. "Ouch!" I put the saucepan down and swiped at my face.

"Careful there, Thatch." Cary said, still stirring. I wondered if he meant to be careful of the hot water, or the interrogation I was subjecting him to. His life was none of my concern, but I'd never met anyone like Cary before. When I was growing up, family and marriage were a big deal. I couldn't even comprehend what my life would've been like if I hadn't met Brian, or if we hadn't had Sam.

I resumed pouring the hot water, and a few moments later we were done. "Keep stirring. See those little lumps?" I pointed at them, and Cary nodded. "We don't want any of those. While you do that, I'll melt the butter in the microwave."

After nuking the butter for thirty seconds, I poured it into the mixture. "Good job, Cary. No more lumps. Now we'll allow it to cool off for five minutes."

"Are you one of those people who thinks there is someone out there for everyone?" Cary asked. "A diehard romantic who lives in a fantasy world of pure, one-hundred-percent true love?"

I was about to answer him when the buzzer from the gate sounded. "Be right back." When I got to the intercom, I pressed the button and spoke. "How may I help you?"

"Hey, this is Joey Davies, the nurse. I'm supposed to check on Cary Lancaster every day." He said, and I flipped on the security camera to double check it was him.

"C'mon in." I said, pressing a button so the gate would open. I dashed back into the kitchen. "Your nurse is here. Stay put, and I'll bring him to you."

A minute later, a blue Prius parked in front of the house. The nurse got out of his car and waved when I opened the front door. "Hi, Mr. Fuller."

The nurse was in his street clothes, wearing a pair of jeans and a blue and green flannel shirt. "You can call me Thatch." I said, and let him into the house. He was carrying a beat-up-leather backpack that I assumed was filled with medical supplies. "Your patient is in the kitchen helping me prepare supper."

"Why is he out of bed?" Joey asked. "He's not strong enough to be walking around."

"You've met our patient already. Would you expect him to do anything he's instructed to do?" I barked out a laugh. "He's damned impossible to deal with."

"No I'm not." Cary said as we entered the kitchen. "I managed the journey from upstairs just fine, thank you very much."

"No, he didn't." I sighed. "When I came across him, his ass was planted on the stairs."

"Tattletale." Cary stuck out his tongue, then yawned. "You can't expect me to stay in bed for the rest of my life."

"No, but I expect you to stay in it until you've regained your strength." Joey opened his backpack and pulled out a stetho-scope. "Open your shirt for me, Mr. Lancaster."

While Joey examined Cary, I took over the making of the spoon bread. Swear to everything holy that looking after Cary was more difficult than looking after Sam when he was a toddler. But I had to admit, he had a certain charisma, and a fuck-all attitude that probably turned on any guy under the age of thirty. It was appealing, in an adorable way. But a man like him would drive me to do some serious drinking. Not that I had to worry about it, since in Cary's eyes I was an ancient, doddering old-timer on the verge of entering a nursing home. He thought I was fifty-one going on a hundred, and in my opinion, he was forty-nine going on twelve.

"Do you need me to help you back up the stairs, Mr. Lancaster?" Joey asked.

"No." Cary grimaced. "I've never been sick with more than a cold in my life. Being ill sucks."

"It's a fact of life, Cary. Happens to the best of us." I said, then slid the spoon bread into the oven.

"Whatever you're making smells like heaven." Joey grinned at me and winked. Cary noticed and rolled his eyes. "Let me get going then." He put his supplies in the backpack and zipped it up.

"Did you want to stay for supper?" I asked. "There's more than enough."

Joey hesitated, then replied. "I wish I could, but Mom insisted I have dinner with her and my grandparents. Poppy just got out of the hospital a few days ago, and Mom wants us to spend more time with him."

"Poppy?" Cary lifted an eyebrow.

"That's what all of us call my grandfather. He's seventy-nine this year, and his health hasn't been what it used to be. I want to spend as much time with him as I can." Joey said, and threw his backpack over his shoulder. "But I will take a raincheck."

"It's a deal. If you show up around the same time tomorrow, I'll likely have supper ready. Thanks for helping us out."

"Look forward to it. I can let myself out." Joey winked at me again and left.

"That guy thinks you're hot stuff." Cary said, once we heard the front door shut. "You should go for it."

"Him?" I laughed. "Joey's too young. He can't be a day over thirty, and he's more interested in me, the writer, than who I really am." I pulled two plates out of the cupboard and set one in front of Cary.

"You know what your problem is?" Cary asked.

"You." I waggled my eyebrows, and he laughed.

"I deserve that. My parents went through so many nannies, and each one of them said the same thing. They couldn't keep up with me. Anyhow, your problem is you have a narrow, conservative view of men and relationships. So what if he's younger? It's not like you have to marry him or something."

"Cary, let's…" I stared up at the ceiling for a moment, and I realized he might be right. I had an appointment to see my old therapist in a couple of days. Maybe I should talk about this when I see her. I glanced up and the timer on the oven dinged, so I used it as an excuse to change the subject. "Supper's just about…"

"Do whatever makes you happy, dude." Cary laid his hand on mine for a moment, then patted my arm. "Just remember, life is fucking short. Ask me how I know."

CHAPTER 12
THATCH

After Joey left yesterday, Cary had quieted down. I suspected he wasn't the type of man given to introspection, but his health scare had to be inspiring some soul-searching. After getting him back upstairs and tucked into bed, he'd fallen asleep the moment his head hit the pillow. When I brought him some oatmeal and juice for breakfast, all he'd said was thanks, and could he have coffee too?

Now it was noon, and his silence was becoming suspicious. He had my cell number and knew to text me whenever he needed something, but so far, nada. And the most disturbing part of his silence was that I actually missed talking to him. Like, what the hell was wrong with me?

"I need a man like Cary the same way I need writer's block." I grumbled as I placed his lunch on a tray. "Not that he's remotely interested in me."

My eyes caught my reflection in the shiny refrigerator. I'd always liked my gray hair, and how it made me feel mature and responsible. Now I felt like a gnarly old man that no one would ever find desirable.

When I see my therapist Cris tomorrow, maybe she'll help me deal with this bullshit, or at the very least, help me transition into a state of acceptance, because this isn't healthy.

With a sigh, I lifted the tray and headed for the stairs. Cary had scarfed down supper last night, so I had heaped his plate with leftovers. Spoon bread, green beans, and cold fried chicken would cheer him up, though why I was worrying about his state of mind made little sense. I needed him to get healthy, so he would get the hell out of my house.

I knocked on the door to Sam's room and opened it. Cary was sitting up in bed with no shirt on, scratching his skin.

"Lunch is here." I crossed the room and placed the tray on his lap, and sweet tea on the nightstand. "Is something wrong?"

"No, why do you ask?" He continued scratching.

"Are you itchy? Do I need to get you some calamine lotion?" He was relatively fit, and if he didn't have a chest full of red scratch marks, I'd be a little turned on.

"No, don't bother. My hair is growing back, and it's driving me crazy." Cary gripped the sheets, presumably to control his scratching.

"I'm confused," I blinked. "You are talking about the hair on your chest, right?" His skin was smooth, but when I leaned over for a closer look, I noticed gray stubble on his pecs. Cary crossed his arms over his chest and glared at me.

"I usually keep it waxed clean. But now that I'm, well, off the dating scene, I'm letting it grow back." He said, then gazed down at the tray. "Ooh, yummy. The spoon bread is awesome."

"Ouch!" My hands clutched my chest. "Why did you wax your chest?"

Cary frowned. "Because boys liked it. Now, if you'll excuse me, I want to eat this tasty meal you've prepared, and as always, I'm very grateful."

He unfolded the napkin on the tray and set it next to him. I didn't want to hover over him while he ate, so I turned and went to the door.

"Thatch," Cary said, and I spun around.

"Yes."

"I'm not feeling well today, so when Joey arrives, send him up here." Cary took a sip of tea and made a face. "Good God, this is sweet."

"Is everything okay? Are you sure you don't want to come downstairs? You told me yesterday that you were losing your mind up here." What the hell was wrong with me? Cary staying out of my hair was a good thing.

"I'm fine, just tired. Now, let me eat in peace." Cary picked up a piece of chicken, so I turned around and as I walked through the door, he piped up, "Enjoy your dinner with Joey."

———

A few minutes past five, I heard the buzz of the security gate, so I opened it and waited by the front door for Joey to arrive. It was strange, because I had the distinct feeling that Cary was trying to play matchmaker with me and the nurse. If Joey wasn't coming over, I guessed Cary would've come downstairs and pestered me for most of the day.

"Hi, Mr. Fuller." Joey grinned as he stepped out of his car. He swung his leather bag over his shoulder and walked toward me. "How's our patient today?"

"Please, call me Thatch." I shut the door behind us, walked to the foot of the stairs and gestured for him to go up. "Cary hasn't left his room all day. Said he was feeling tired."

"Are we still on for supper? Because I can smell something delicious coming from your kitchen." Joey's hair was pulled back into a ponytail, similar to how I used to keep my hair when it was still full and dark.

"If you love field peas, buttermilk biscuits, and pan-fried steak, you will love your supper." I smiled and felt my stomach rumble. It was nerves or hunger, I couldn't tell which.

"Are you feeding that to Cary? Because it sounds delicious, but he shouldn't be eating rich foods right now." Joey opened his leather bag and rifled through it, then pulled out a piece of paper. "These are the foods he should minimize. Anything fried, or fatty."

"Oh, he didn't get the same meal we are having. Cary requested a Greek salad with lots of feta cheese and kalamata olives. I took his meal up to him half-an-hour ago." When I did, he'd told me to go to my room and change my shirt. I'd said nothing and kept my shirt on. Didn't have a clue why he'd tell me that.

"Well, this shouldn't take too long. I'll be back down in a flash." Joey winked, then headed up the stairs.

———

"Did you know Cary snuck a salt shaker into his room? Or did you put it on his tray?" Joey said, then placed a spoonful of field peas in his mouth.

"I must have put it on his tray by accident. Though he spent an awful lot of time in the kitchen yesterday. I thought his heart was okay. Why is salt bad for him?"

Joey sipped his tea, then answered. "Yeah, he didn't have a heart attack, but he has issues with cholesterol and his blood pressure is slightly elevated. For right now, keep salty and fatty foods to a minimum."

"Yes, sir." I cut up my steak. "How was your patient?"

"Our patient," Joey chuckled, "...is, well, a piece of work.

When I was checking out his heart with the stethoscope, I noticed all these scratch marks, and asked what was wrong with his skin. I can't believe he'd been waxing the hair on his chest, plus he was doing it to his back and his crotch."

I shuddered, and Joey laughed.

"That's got to hurt. Did you ask him why?" Even though I already knew the answer, I wondered if Cary would 'fess up to Joey.

"Yes, he was very forthcoming about it. Said the young guys prefer men to be smooth, so every three weeks he'd pop some pain pills and go to the salon. That's when I asked if he was into BDSM." Joey pressed his lips together.

"Oh my God," I cracked up, and so did he. Once I got my laughter under control, I asked, "So, what was his answer?"

"Cary replied that while he'd spank anyone who asked for it, it wasn't his thing." Joey sipped his tea and frowned. "He said he was a romantic, that he wasn't all that into sex games and stuff. That totally threw me, because I thought he was a horn dog, not a romantic."

"Yeah, I'm kind of surprised by that answer, too."

"You want to know what else we talked about?" Joey pushed his plate to the side, then reached over and took my hand. No man had held my hand since Brian left me, and I prayed it wasn't clammy. I nodded, unable to speak for a moment.

"You. He said you've been lonely since your divorce, and that I should officially ask you out on a date."

Sweat dripped down my sides as my heart pounded.

"So, Thatch, will you come with me to a bluegrass festival on Saturday? I don't know if that's your thing, but if it isn't, we can do whatever you want." Joey bit his lower lip, waiting for my response.

I didn't know what to say. Live music was great, but I

wasn't sure if I felt attracted to him or not. It had been so long since I'd been on a proper date, and well, it frightened me. Joey's eyebrows drew together, and his grip on my hand tightened.

"Is this a yes or a no?"

CHAPTER 13

CARY

"Jenny, overnight those papers so I can sign them, then email me the blueprints Mr. Prentiss sent you. If it's feasible, I'd like to purchase his building, but only if we can get him to drop the price." I shut my eyes, imagining what my proposed art gallery in downtown Raleigh would look like. "Why don't you invite him out to lunch, and use your considerable charm to make him easier to… well, work with." I hated using the word manipulate, which was more accurate.

"No problem, Cary. And since he's a muscled hottie, I'll even bend over backwards to get him to see things our way, if you get my drift." Jenny purred, and I chuckled.

"Isn't he a little old for you?" I asked, and puffed on a contraband cigar, blowing the smoke out the window.

"He's your age, Cary. I happen to like a seasoned man. They don't need a fucking map to find my…"

"I understand," I cut her off before the conversation turned x-rated. "You do whatever you feel is appropriate, but remember, it's your choice if the negotiations end up in the bedroom, and not the boardroom."

THE CAD AND DAD 83

"Did I tell you I think the man you're staying with is hot? If he didn't play for your team, I'd be on him in a heartbeat." Jenny giggled, and I was rendered momentarily speechless. I mean, Thatch was a handsome guy, but he was my age.

"Are you still there, Cary?"

"Yes, sorry, I..." The sound of a throat clearing startled me. I glanced up and saw the current topic of conversation standing in the doorway with a scowl. "Jenny, I've got to go. Thatch wants something."

"It's almost midnight. Please, tell me he's standing in front of you in his underwear." Jenny breathed, and I disconnected the call. He had a plaid flannel robe on, and for a split-second I wondered what he looked like in his underwear. Boxers? Briefs? Commando?

"What is that?" Thatch pointed in my direction and I realized he meant the cigar.

"Shit, I'm sorry." I'd turned a saucer into an ashtray and stubbed it out. Thatch crossed the room and took it out of my hand.

"I can't... damn it, Cary. It's not my job to be your nurse, but if you keep smoking these things, you'll end up in the hospital again. Please, stop being the bad-boy patient. It's undignified. Do what Joey tells you, and soon you'll be driving that pretty Rolls Royce back to Raleigh where you can fuck up your health all you want." Thatch barked. He was a couple of inches taller than me, and for the first time since we met I felt vaguely intimidated by him.

"It won't happen again." I crossed the room and sat on the corner of the bed.

"I hate the smell of smoke, and cigars are the worst. Where's your stash?" Thatch held his hand out.

"Damn it," I muttered, and pointed at the dresser. "Bottom drawer on the right."

Thatch opened it and took the last few cigars I had left, then he crossed the room and opened every single window.

"May I ask you something?"

Thatch stared at me and said nothing for a moment.

"Have you always been like this? Or do I bring it out in you?"

Thatch continued to stare at me, not speaking.

"Because, I don't think I've ever had this effect on a man before. Most guys like me, think I'm a charmer, but you obviously dislike me, and I don't know what I can do to change that." I fell back on the mattress and stared at the ceiling.

"What effect do you think you have on me?" Thatch asked, and I forced myself to sit up, so I could see his face.

"I'm not sure, but I'm not used to having someone blow so hot and cold. One minute you're teaching me how to cook, and everything feels great. The next minute you're treating me like a teenage boy who…"

"Because, you're acting like a child." Thatch muttered, rolling his eyes. He walked over to the nightstand, picked up the empty tray from dinner and piled my cigars and the saucer on it.

"You don't sleep much, do you?" I asked, wondering if he was an insomniac like me. It might explain his pissy attitude.

"I only need five hours or so. I would be asleep right now, but the smell of lung cancer jolted me awake." Thatch sighed, and his features softened. "So, who were you talking to at this hour?"

"My assistant, Jenny. Oh, and she thinks you're hot." I winked, and was delighted to see his already pink face turn a deeper shade of red. "She asked me if you were in your underwear."

"Jesus Christ." Thatch shook his head. "She's as bad as you. Goodnight, Cary."

———

For the next two hours, I struggled to keep my eyes shut, but sleep wouldn't come. When my stomach grumbled, I debated if I should venture a trip to the kitchen. There might be some of that spoon bread left.

"I can do it." I pushed the blankets off me and swung my feet to the floor. "Just take it slow, and I'll be fine."

A moment later, I put my robe on and inched the bedroom door open. I padded down the hall, occasionally stopping to catch my breath. Walking was easier now than it was a couple of days ago, but it still took effort. When I turned the corner where the master bedroom and the staircase were, I noticed the bedroom door was open. A soft light shone on the hardwood floor, and I prayed Thatch wasn't awake. When I got to his door, Thatch howled.

"Oh my God! What are you doing up?!"

Startled, I slammed against the opposite wall, then fell to my knees. "Ouch!"

Thatch was standing in the middle of his bedroom, scrambling to get his robe on. Apparently, I wasn't the only one who enjoyed sleeping in the nude.

"Oh, I'm so sorry, Thatch." I turned away, but the image of his naked body was burnt into my brain. When I rose to my feet, I muttered, "Jesus, what was I thinking?"

I made it to the staircase and was about to ease my way down when Thatch came flying out of his room and grabbed my arm.

"It's two in the morning. Why are you out of bed?"

I couldn't meet his gaze, but when I looked down, all I could think about was the healthy size of Thatch's package. Blood raced up my neck, and to my surprise, below my waist.

"Hungry, um, I was going to the kitchen." I couldn't look

Thatch in the face, or anywhere else, for that matter. "I'm sorry, I got confused, um, uh, I didn't really see anything, but…"

"You've seen one dick, you've seen them all." Thatch sighed and stared up at the ceiling. "It's not a big deal, Cary."

I wanted to say that yes, it was quite a big deal, but had a feeling that it wouldn't come out right. "I'll go back to bed. Sorry, Thatch."

"No, no. I could use a little snack myself." Thatch shook his head and smiled. "Let's go to the kitchen, you peeping Tom."

———

"Here," Thatch slid a bowl of what looked like soggy, brown peanuts in their shells in front of me.

"What are these?"

"Boiled peanuts. They are the best snack on God's green earth. Try one." Thatch stared at me expectantly, so I snatched one out of the bowl, and popped it in my mouth. It tasted awful, like moist bark. I spit it into my hand instead.

"That was revolting."

"Bless your heart, Cary, take the shell off the nut first, like this." Thatch grabbed a peanut, pinched the middle of the shell and it broke apart, leaving what appeared to be beans. I cleaned my hand with a napkin, then picked up a peanut, mimicked Thatch and popped the beans in my mouth.

"Oh wow," I groaned. "These are amazing." I grabbed another one, shelled it, and popped them in my mouth. "I'm addicted to salty foods, and these are wonderful."

"Damn it. I forgot, you're supposed to keep salty foods to a minimum." Thatch moved to take the boiled peanuts away, but I laid my hand on top of the bowl.

"No."

"Fine," Thatch chuckled, and began eating the peanuts with

me. We ate in silence for a few minutes, then I remembered what I'd told my nurse Joey when I saw him last.

"So, did Joey ask you out?"

Thatch sighed. "Yes, he did."

"And?"

Thatch thought for a moment, then gripped the counter and eyed me. "I didn't give him an answer."

"Why? It's obvious he likes you." This man confused the hell out of me. It was like he wanted to be alone. I had no choice in the matter, now that my health was sketchy, but Thatch had an attractive thirty-something begging for a piece of him.

"Since you are leaving soon, I'll tell you why." Thatch combed his wavy gray hair off his face and frowned. "I want to talk to my therapist first, before giving him an answer."

"Why do you need a shrink? You're not crazy."

"It's, well, complicated. Are you done with these?" Thatch gestured toward the bowl of peanuts. I nodded, and he put a plastic lid on the bowl and stuck it in the fridge. "Let's get you back to bed."

———

Once Thatch switched off the overhead light and shut the door, my imagination went into overdrive, trying to imagine what Thatch had looked like in his twenties. Dark hair like Sam, and with long, lean limbs that would pin you down while…

"Stop it." I groaned, and rolled onto my stomach. Getting worked up when my health was on the fritz wasn't a bright idea. Now my head was filled with the image of Thatch naked in front of me, and I had to admit, he was one helluva handsome guy, even if he was old. Barely an ounce of fat, and while he was thin, he had defined muscles that he had to be hiding on purpose. "Probably why he's always in jeans, and loose fitting shirts. Dude needs to flaunt it, not conceal it."

I flipped over onto my back, then switched on the lamp. One hand snaked under the blanket and gripped my semi. "What the hell is wrong with this picture? Am I really getting turned on by a man even older than me?"

CHAPTER 14

THATCH

"I'm going into town for a few hours. Are you going to be okay by yourself?"

"Yes, I've got plenty to keep myself busy." Cary pointed at his laptop, then gestured toward the papers covering the bed. Every day his assistant sent more of his work here, which worried me. Like, would he ever leave my house?

"Text me if you need anything."

I turned to go and he spoke. "Where are you going?"

"Well, if you must know, I've an appointment with my therapist." Why I felt compelled to tell him the truth baffled me. I should have said anything but that. Cary's eyes widened, and a slow smile spread across his cheeks.

"I've already told you that you don't need a shrink. You're as sane and steady as they come, Thatch." Cary said, and I noticed something different in his eyes. If I wasn't mistaken, he actually cared about me, or at the very least he was an excellent actor.

"Thank you, Cary. But every once in a while it's good for me to check in with her. She gives me a different perspective on things, and right now I could use that." I said, then turned to leave, but Cary spoke again.

"If you ever want to talk, I'm all ears."

———

I'd first gone to see Cris Foster when Brian filed for divorce. She'd had a calming effect on me, and helped me realize that I was in charge of my emotional well-being, not my ex-husband. Before I started therapy, I thought seeing a therapist was a waste of time. What kept me going back to her was silly, but I was glad I stuck it out. Her name was the same as my favorite character on The Young And The Restless, a soap opera my granny and I watched together when I was a kid. It was a stupid reason, but watching the stories, as my granny called them, was the beginning of my love affair with telling stories of my own.

Blue Ridge Pride Behavioral Associates was in a plain, one-story brick house on the other side of Asheville. There were only three therapists and a receptionist. A trans friend who found their help invaluable had referred me to them as he was transitioning. After three years of weekly visits I announced that I felt healed enough to stop coming. Now I was back with my tail between my legs.

As I stepped out of my SUV onto the gravel driveway, the front door opened and a woman stepped out, tears streaming down her face. My first instinct was to comfort her, but when she saw me she covered her face with her hand and ran to her car.

"God, am I so confused about my life that I want to reopen old wounds?" I muttered, then forced myself to move. Suddenly, I remembered being that woman. Reliving every drama Brian and I had gone through. But, it was worth it in the end. We might have been divorced, but Brian and I kept our friendship and business arrangements going, thanks to Cris.

"Thatch, it's good to see you again!" The receptionist said when I walked through the door. His name was Tim, and he also taught yoga and reiki at the new age bookstore downtown.

"Hey Tim." I grinned. When I was about to sit on the tattered overstuffed sofa, he stopped me.

"Thatch, I forgot to ask you this on the phone. Are you allergic to dogs? Because Cris now has an emotional support dog that sits in on the sessions."

"Oh, really? I love dogs. Can't wait to meet..."

"Her name is Harmony, and you'll love her. She's been helpful for certain patients, and hopefully Harmony will be a comfort to you as well." Tim said, then placed his hands together like he was praying, and bowed his head. "Cris is ready for you."

"Oh, that was fast," I replied. "Is she still in the same office?"

"Cris's office is at the end of the hallway, the one with the dreamcatcher hanging on the door." He pointed toward her office. "Just walk on in, she's expecting you."

Hanging from her door was a hoop with what appeared to be crude netting inside of it. Bird feathers and brightly colored beads were woven into it. When I opened the door it appeared smoky inside, and an overpowering smell of musk roared up my nostrils.

"Thatch, it's lovely to see you again." Cris beamed at me, and then I saw the source of the smoke. Incense was burning in an elaborate brass thingy, and I recalled how Cris always kept it burning, saying it helped cleanse the spirit.

"You look the same," I commented. Her long brown hair was in a single braid hanging over her left shoulder, and she still had the same granny glasses, similar to the ones John Lennon wore. I held out my hand and she took it in hers, but instead of shaking it, she held it in both hands and shut her eyes.

"I can sense your anxiety," Cris murmured, then opened her eyes and released my hand. "You're in a safe space. Let's begin the healing process." She gestured toward the blue velvet antique couch across from her desk, so I sat. "Let me introduce you to the newest member of Blue Ridge Pride Behavioral Associates, Harmony."

A gorgeous long-haired black chihuahua crawled out from under the couch and stared at me. "Go ahead," Cris directed me. "Pick her up. She loves cuddles."

I leaned over and set her on my lap. Then the little darling got on her hind feet with her paws on my chest and licked my chin. "Aww, what a sweet girl." After the kiss, Harmony curled up on my lap. "What a wonderful way to put your clients at ease."

"Harmony is a rescue. My wife Amber found her at the animal shelter and couldn't resist bringing her home." Amber was one of the therapists working here. "Normally she lives up to her name, but today she got a little feisty with me."

"It's hard to believe this little bundle of fluff could be a bad girl." I cooed while Harmony licked my fingers.

"It's understandable why, so all is forgiven. The vet cancelled her appointment today, so I had to go on YouTube and look up videos on how to express a dog's anal gland." She threw her hands up in the air. "Poor Harmony was past due for it. I managed to get the job done, and saved a ton of money too."

I glanced down at my hands, the ones Cris had just held in her own. Harmony tilted her tiny head, a questioning look in her eyes. I scanned the room, praying there was a bottle of hand sanitizer somewhere, but there wasn't.

"It was a lot more difficult than I thought. But Harmony is a trooper. So what's going on with you, Thatch?" Cris asked, picking lint from the sleeve of her lavender turtleneck. "The last time we spoke you felt at peace with your ex-husband."

It took a moment for me to get my thoughts together. On the ride here I'd gone over everything I wanted to say, but after learning about Harmony's anal gland it had all flown out of my head.

Cris stared at me with a neutral expression that had always made me feel like I wasn't being judged, while I struggled to get my brain to work. "Dating. Men. Um, there's something wrong with me." I mumbled.

"Go on." Cris murmured, her eyes not leaving mine. "Remember, this is a safe space. Feel free to share whatever you need to."

"I'm fifty-one years old, and I've been divorced for several years. But in all that time I haven't gone on a single date. Finally, a man asked me out, and I'm terrified." I blurted, and Harmony dug into my crotch with her rear leg.

"How does this man make you feel?"

I nudged Harmony to get her to stop kicking my junk, shut my eyes and pictured Joey's face. "He's handsome, with shoulder-length brown hair, and he works as a nurse. But, he's much younger than I am."

"I asked how you felt about him, but you still said something interesting. Do you have issues with this age gap?" Cris asked, and I waved a cloud of smoke out of my face.

"Well, yeah. In my head I know it shouldn't be a problem, but..."

"But, it is." Cris said, a nun's smile settling on her face. "Are you attracted to this man?"

"Kind of?" I mumbled. What did I think about him? It wasn't like I was gaga over Joey. "When I met Brian, my ex-husband, I immediately felt something for him." I laced my fingers through Harmony's hair and began stroking her. "Actually, Brian pissed me off when we first met, but I can't remember what it was."

Cris raised an eyebrow.

"Oh, I remember. It was his attitude. A few weeks later and I couldn't imagine life without him, but Joey is different. He's very nice, good-looking, and, you know, nice." I shrugged my shoulders, wishing I could explain the doubt I felt. Hell, I was a best-selling author, but the correct words escaped me.

"Something is holding you back, right?" Cris asked, then pointed at the coffee table in front of me. "See that piece of obsidian?"

"Um, what is that?"

"It's that shiny piece of black glass. Pick it up and hold it in your hands." I did as instructed, and Harmony growled when I bent over. "Obsidian is a crystal that aids in healing. It possesses energies that help you process emotions. Can you feel the power?"

It felt heavy and smooth, but that was about it. I nodded yes anyway. Who knows? Maybe it was doing something and I was too skeptical to feel it.

"Close your eyes, Thatch."

I did as instructed, and was startled when I heard what sounded like a gong.

"Focus, Thatch." Cris's voice deepened. "How do you actually feel about the man who asked you on a date?"

"Nothing," I blurted. "Like, he's a nice guy, but I feel nothing. He's taking care of the pain in my ass that's living upstairs, so I guess I feel gratitude for his, um, presence."

"You just mentioned that a so-called pain in the ass is living upstairs from you." Cris said, and I opened my eyes. "I'm assuming it means a person."

I nodded.

"Does this person have a name?" Cris asked, and I realized I was still rubbing the stupid glass rock. I set it back on the coffee table, and Harmony growled again.

"Cary Lancaster," I sighed. "He's this guy my son brought home." How the hell could I describe this man and the chaos he'd brought to my life? "To make a long story short, Cary had a medical emergency and he's recuperating in Sam's bedroom. I would send him packing, but his doctor insists on keeping him close by the hospital."

Cris steepled her hands under her chin and shut her eyes for a moment. When she opened them, she asked, "So, this man infuriates you?"

"God yes. Cary is a pompous, stuck-up rich guy who thinks the world revolves around him. He even drives a Rolls Royce. Like, who the hell does that unless you want to flaunt your privilege to the world?" I snapped.

Harmony yipped, then jumped off my lap and scampered under the couch. Cris scribbled something, then pursed her lips. She opened her mouth, shut it again, then spoke.

"Maybe you should reconsider why you are here, Thatch, because it sounds to me like Cary is the source of your angst."

CHAPTER 15

CARY

"How did things go with Mr. Prentiss?" I asked Jenny, who yawned.

"Sorry, but he kept me out half the night, but it was totally worth it. I think I can get him to shave off a few thousand on the final asking price." She said proudly. "I didn't even have to fuck him."

I clucked my tongue. "You never have to sleep with anyone we work with, Jenny."

"But, that's half the fun," she said in a singsong voice. "It turns out he's engaged to be married to some dowdy, matronly woman. He showed me a picture of her, and she's a real bow wow."

"Love is blind, sweetie. So tell me, how did you charm him?"

"Well, all I had to do was make it obvious to him that I wanted a roll in the hay. His ego exploded, but he was able to maintain his virtue. It's always weird to meet a straight guy who doesn't want to get laid." Jenny sighed.

"Stop stereotyping them. Not every straight guy is an

asshole." I said, then heard a knock at the door. "Jenny, gotta go. Talk to you tomorrow, oh, and thanks for taking care of Mr. Prentiss. Excellent work." I hung up the phone, and called out, "Come in."

"Wow, you have real clothes on." Joey said as he strolled over to the bed. "What's the occasion?"

"I was bored with loungewear, so my assistant sent me a couple of outfits. You like?" I grinned rakishly and winked.

Joey laughed. "Your outfit probably costs what I make in a week, but I have to admit, this nautical look suits you."

I was wearing a white t-shirt with a navy-blue and white striped sweater draped over my shoulders, and matching blue slacks. "Thank you, sir." I glanced down at my phone and saw he was here earlier than usual.

Joey sat on the edge of the bed. "Dr. Creighton will be here any minute. She wants to see if you're healthy enough to travel."

"Do you think I'm ready? Because I'm definitely feeling better." I bit my lip. "Overstaying my welcome isn't something I normally do."

"The doctor is making that decision. Are you still having dizzy spells?" Joey opened his bag and pulled out his tablet.

"Not as much," I lied. Being ill was a state of being I loathed. I'd always been busy, and being stuck in Thatch's house when he obviously didn't want me here made me very uncomfortable. "So, what's going on with you and Thatch?"

Joey let out a lengthy sigh, almost a groan. "Still hasn't said yes to going out with me. I honestly don't know what to do."

"Well, after spending far too much time in his house, I can accurately tell you he's a little uptight, so much so that it's funny to watch. Maybe it's for the best that he hasn't said yes." Why the hell did I just say that? I wanted Thatch to loosen up and go out with Joey. Joey would be perfect for him, especially if he wanted a fun fling with a younger man.

"How's your breathing? Still having trouble catching your breath?"

"Thatch threw out my cigars, so yes, it's been easier to breathe." I rolled my eyes. "He also introduced me to boiled peanuts, and I must say they were mighty tasty."

"You shouldn't be eating salty foods." Joey shook his head and typed something into the tablet.

"I saw Thatch naked." I didn't know why that flew out of my mouth. Possibly because I couldn't stop thinking about it.

"That doesn't sound very uptight to me." Joey muttered, and I noticed his jaw clench.

"It was an accident."

Joey glared at me, then his features softened. "Okay. Indulge my curiosity. How did you see him naked by accident?"

"It was close to two in the morning and I was hungry, so I attempted the stairs by myself, hoping to score more spoon bread in the kitchen. The staircase is next to Thatch's room, and his door was open." I shut my eyes, and the image of his lean, muscled body filled my head.

"And?"

"When he saw me he screamed, you know, because he's uptight. Then he helped me down the stairs, and we ate peanuts together." I noticed Joey's usual cheerful face was now looking downright sullen. And the sick thing was, I was getting off on making him jealous. There was absolutely no future for me and Thatch, but oddly enough, I now couldn't bear the thought of Joey going out with him. I shut my eyes and rubbed my temples, confused.

"Did he put some clothes on, you know, before helping you to the kitchen?" Joey said, leaning closer to me.

"Of course," I smiled. Then, Dr. Creighton strolled into the room followed by Thack, who was only wearing a red tank top and running shorts. I'd never seen him in workout gear, and my eyes were glued to his every movement.

"How's my patient today?" Dr. Creighton smiled, and I was pleased to see she was wearing the pearls I'd bought for her.

"Great, couldn't be better. I think I should be able to leave soon." I grinned, trying to observe Thatch out of the corner of my eye without being caught.

"Cary says he's not feeling as dizzy, and he's been getting a lot of rest." Joey said, a hopeful tone to his voice. He didn't sound like that just a minute ago, and I wondered if he was trying to get me out of the house.

"Let me listen to your heart." Dr. Creighton pulled a stethoscope out of her black doctor's bag. "I hate to ask you this, but would you mind lifting your shirt for a moment?"

"Sure," I replied, sneaking another glance at Thatch. I shrugged the sweater off my shoulders, then raised my shirt up to my neck. When the ice-cold stethoscope made contact with my skin, I flinched.

"Sorry about that. I know it's cold." Dr. Creighton said, then I noticed Thatch bending over and picking something up from the floor. "Your heart is racing, Cary."

"I don't know why," I muttered, and when Thatch settled back against the dresser again, his bulge was very obvious through his running shorts.

"Have you been taking your meds?" Dr. Creighton dropped the stethoscope on the bed next to her and grabbed my wrist. "There's something going on, because your pulse is so fast it's almost like you've run a marathon." She dropped my wrist, and I noticed a scowl on Joey's face.

"Dr. Creighton, I must return to Raleigh soon. My business is…"

"You aren't going anywhere for at least another week, not

with the stress your heart is under." She shook her head and turned to Thatch. "I know this has been difficult for you, but can you bear to keep Cary here a while longer?"

Dr. Creighton stood up and faced Thatch, who smiled.

"What's another week or two?" He said, and sat where the doctor had been a moment earlier. "You're kinda growing on me, Cary. Let's get you healthy so you can go home."

———

After they all left, I turned off the lights, got in bed, and screamed into my pillow. This situation was becoming impossible. For some reason, I now had the hots for Thatch, and if he hadn't been in the room when Dr. Creighton was here, I was positive my heart would have been beating normally.

"If Thatch is going to walk around the house wearing practically nothing, I'll never get out of here."

How could I explain to the doctor in front of Thatch and Joey that my heart started beating out of control at the sight of Thatch? It would not have set well with my host, or with the nurse who had a crush on the same guy I did. And the thing was, it was better for all involved if I bowed out gracefully and went back to my own life. Dating was out of the question now that my health wasn't up to snuff. And maybe Thatch was right. My dating younger men was probably off the table for good, too.

"Late nights at clubs?" I sighed. "No more. Keeping up with twenty-somethings? Definitely not."

There was a knock at the door. "You decent Cary?" Thatch asked.

"Come on in." I said, hoping Thatch was wearing his usual clothes that covered everything. When the door opened, I sighed with relief. He was back in jeans and a red and white striped button-down shirt.

"Hey, I know you wanted to get out of here." Thatch said, then he sat down next to me on the bed. "But, sometimes you just have to rest and heal."

"I'm sick of resting."

"You have every reason to want to leave. It must be difficult being cooped up in here, plus this health scare is probably provoking some inner reflection, which can't be easy." Thatch patted me on the knee, and I felt my cock thicken.

Stop touching me. For the love of God, stop.

Frantically, I thought of ways to get him to leave.

"Um, so how did it go with your shrink?" I asked, hoping the question would make him uncomfortable.

"It went well." Thatch stood and started pacing around the room. I noticed he didn't like to sit still for long, which was how I used to be when I was healthy. "We ended up talking about you."

"Me?" Shit, that couldn't be good.

"I'm sorry for my behavior, Cary. When I discovered you were dating Sam, it freaked me out, but my son is a grown man, and I have to get on with my life." Thatch strolled over to the windows and opened the curtains. "You should enjoy the sunshine, especially since you haven't been outside for so long."

"Thanks," I mumbled.

"My therapist also helped me see things differently with dating and men. I kind of don't trust guys easily, and maybe I've been selling myself short." Thatch stood at the end of the bed and grinned down at me. "So, I accepted Joey's offer to go on a date."

Damn it.

"Are you okay? Because your face lost all of its color." Thatch tilted his head.

"Yeah, sure." I forced myself to smile. "Would you mind leaving? I'm not feeling well. Perhaps I should take a nap."

"Okay." Thatch went to the door, then turned around. "I'm making a vegetable stir fry for dinner. It's from a heart-healthy cookbook Joey loaned me. Do you want to come downstairs later, or should I bring it up to you on a tray?"

"Just leave the tray outside my door." I turned my head and gazed out the window. "Have a great time with Joey."

Silence.

I wondered if Thatch was still there, then I heard the door open, and shut.

"Fuck."

CHAPTER 16

THATCH

"I can't believe I'm going on a date." I hopped up and down for a moment, then realized how foolish I was being. Even if things didn't work out between Joey and me, and I suspected they wouldn't, at least I was putting myself out there.

I was excited, and it was reflected in my work. Instead of struggling to get words on paper, they were flowing like the waterfall outside my office window, and from what I could see, this wasn't a shitty first draft. It was clean, concise, and sounded natural when I spoke the words aloud.

It was nine in the morning, and I'd only had one cup of coffee. I got up from my desk and was about to make a second cup in the little kitchenette, when a stab of guilt tore through me.

Cary was alone. No family. His friends, if he had any, weren't here. I'd done my research online, and his contact list must be a who's who of famous artists. Had he not reached out to them while he was sick? Or worse still, did they not give a damn?

When we first met, I couldn't stand the man, but what I said the other day was true. Cary was growing on me, and when I saw the look on his face after announcing I was going out with Joey, it almost made me reconsider the date. The thing was, I couldn't understand why he appeared so glum about it. Suddenly, the reason for his gloomy attitude struck me.

"Does Cary have a thing for Joey?" I smacked my thigh. "That's got to be it."

Joey was younger, and quite handsome, and he'd been an intimate part of Cary's recovery, but out of respect for me, Cary's reluctant host, he was taking himself out of the picture, and that kind, selfless gesture spoke volumes about who Cary was under his layers of grandiosity. He might appear to be a superficial charmer, but I suspected he genuinely cared about me.

Instead of making coffee in my office, I decided to go downstairs and make a big breakfast for the two of us, and I refused to leave the tray outside his door. Cary needed to get out of his room, not hide inside it.

"I reckon turkey bacon is healthier than pork." I pulled a package of it out of the fridge, along with a carton of eggs. A veggie omelet with biscuits on the side would taste great, and if I left out the egg yolks, it would be healthy, too.

"I'm coming downstairs." I heard Cary's voice from upstairs. "If you're naked, put some clothes on!"

I laughed, then wondered if Cary needed help. Leaving the ingredients on the kitchen counter, I headed for the stairs. To my surprise, Cary was halfway down them already, wearing his King of England pajamas.

"You need some help?" I asked, and Cary grinned his brilliant-white smile.

"Look at me, walking around like a healthy guy." His eyes crinkled, and for a split second I wondered why I was going out on a date with Joey, when Cary was the more logical choice. The right age, successful, and if I were being honest with myself, very attractive. "I've decided that fresh air would be good for me. If I'm ever going to get out of your hair, I need to go outside, see the sun."

"That's a splendid idea, Cary." By now, he was at the bottom of the staircase. His descent was slow and steady, unlike the other attempts at the stairs he'd made. "I'm making breakfast. Come join me in the kitchen, and when it's done, we can eat it outside."

Cary strolled into the kitchen, then wobbled a bit when he sat on a stool by the counter. "How can I assist you?"

"Just sit there. Coffee?" I held out an empty mug, and Cary nodded. "I'll put on half a pot."

Cary's color was better today, and even his cheeks had a slight pink tinge. While I scooped the coffee into the wire basket, it felt like he was watching my every movement.

"I already told you I'm over it, you know, your Peeping Tom act. It's not a big deal." I said, filling the coffee maker with water. When I glanced over to Cary, his cheeks were decidedly pinker.

"Well, that's good news. Now I can stop hiding from you." Cary plucked an egg out of the carton and began rolling it around his fingers, almost the way a magician would before making it disappear.

"Oh, so that's why you've been hiding in your room. Cary, I don't want you to feel uncomfortable while you're here. This is an awkward situation for both of us, so let's make the best of it," I sighed. "I am making us both an egg-white veggie omelet with turkey bacon and biscuits. Sound good to you?"

Cary nodded, and again I felt like he was watching my every move. When he'd first arrived, he'd been more talkative, but something had shifted between us. Possibly he was watching what he said, since I was going out with Joey, and he wasn't. "Here." I filled a mug with coffee and placed it in front of him. "Sugar and cream?"

"No, thanks. I drink it black, though if you really look at coffee, it's not black, it's brown." Cary raised his mug and winked. "The better term would be I'll take my coffee plain."

"You've got a point." I filled my mug, then doctored it with a teaspoon of sugar.

"So, where is Joey taking you on your big date?" Cary asked, and his eyes shifted down to his coffee. Was that why he came downstairs? To pump me for information about my date?

"He is taking me to the Bluegrass First Class festival this afternoon. Lots of bands are playing, and it should be fun." I watched Cary as I spoke. His face remained impassive, but he also wasn't meeting my gaze. "I'm not a huge bluegrass fan, but I love live music. Watching the musicians is kind of like watching myself write. They just use different instruments."

"Obviously," Cary muttered, then slowly got to his feet with a groan. "If you don't mind, I'm going to sit outside by the pool. I've missed the great outdoors." He picked up his coffee cup, and walked out the glass door without another word. Cary's gait was slow, but much better.

"I guess you'll be leaving soon," I sighed, and began cracking open the eggs, letting the whites slide through my fingers, then tossing out the yolks. There was something about the man that piqued my curiosity. He was detached from stuff going on around him, and he was also very observant, kind of like he was judging each situation, and the people involved, but refused to become entangled in it, kind of like how writers viewed the world.

"Hm. Maybe we're more alike than I thought."

———

Before I loaded the tray to take it outside, I watched Cary. He was seated at the glass patio table with the blue-and-white umbrella shading him from the sun. His back was to me, and I could see him typing into his phone. That was when I noticed he was barefoot, which was out of character for him. He typically wore black velvet slippers, the kind I'd never spend money on. Was he feeling more relaxed? Or, was I reading too much into things like I usually did?

I opened the glass door, then I poured the rest of the coffee into a carafe, and placed our plates and silverware on the tray. After stepping outside, I gently shut the door with my foot and walked over to where Cary sat. "Breakfast is served."

Cary placed his phone on the table with the screen down and grinned up at me. "Thank you, Thatch. I'm not used to home-cooked meals, and your cooking is outstanding."

"Thank you." I sat down and unfolded a napkin on my lap. "It's one of my favorite hobbies. Here," I handed him a spice blend I'd created the night before. "Try this. It's salt free, but tastes wonderful. Here's some pepper too, if you want it."

When Cary grabbed the shaker of pepper, the sleeve of his robe caught against his coffee cup, spilling it. "Damn it."

"Here, I brought an extra napkin." I began mopping up the spill, and noticed the hot liquid was spreading across the table toward his phone. I grabbed it, mopped up the mess, and when I handed the phone back to him, I could see the screen. It was a search engine, and he'd typed my name into it.

Cary sighed. "There are an awful lot of articles about you." He pointed at the screen. "You've had a fascinating life."

I grinned, then confessed to my own sleuthing. "You're not the only one who's snooped. According to the internet, you've produced a Tony-award-winning show on Broadway, and financed a finalist at the Sundance Film festival. Oh, and sold a publishing company for a healthy profit. Now you prefer a more hands-off approach to investing, according to one of those online finance websites. That's why you are into music streaming and pharmaceuticals now. It's exhausting just reading the amount of stuff you've accomplished."

"Good detective work." Cary crunched a piece of turkey bacon between his teeth.

"Time flies, doesn't it?" I sighed, then sipped my coffee.

"It sure does, but I have very few regrets. When I die, my wiki page will be a lengthy one." Cary grinned and ate the rest of the bacon.

"I have too many regrets to count." I shook my head and noticed how stunning his hair was. It had grown out a bit since he'd arrived, and instead of the short buzz cut he had when he arrived, it was beginning to curl around his ears. Almost boyish, except for the salt and pepper color.

"You are as hard on yourself as you are on others," Cary murmured, then picked up his phone and tapped on the screen. "Fuller is a perfectionist. A writer who methodically turns in an almost perfectly clean first draft every time." He turned the phone around so I could see the quote. My former editor had said this of me in an interview with Publishers Weekly.

It amazed me that he could sense that about me, and better yet, back it up with a source.

"The more I get to know you, the more interesting you are, Cary." I said, and truly meant it. Maybe I should get to know him better? Obviously, he was leaving soon, and his relationship with Sam was over. Though his relationship with my son begged another question, one we'd gone over already, but I doubted Cary had completely answered it.

"What's wrong?" Cary asked. "Sorry if you think I overstepped a boundary by looking you up online."

"No, nothing's wrong," I sighed, then pushed my plate to the side and locked my gaze with his. "Tell me something."

"Sure, ask me anything." Cary slid his phone into the pocket of his robe.

"What's with all the young guys? Like, what's the real reason you've only dated younger men?"

CHAPTER 17

CARY

W hy was Thack insistent on beating a dead horse? It wasn't like I was able to score with twinks anymore. Or anyone else for that matter. That part of my life was over, and now I had to figure out how to fill my days and nights.

Alone.

"Baggage," I sighed.

"Baggage? What on earth does that mean?" Thatch asked, and I found my gaze locking with his blue eyes. They were addictive, and hard to turn away from. I forced myself to focus on the swimming pool.

"You looked me up online, and in case you hadn't noticed, I was a busy guy. I dated twinks because the older you are, the more experiences you've had. Whether those experiences are good or bad, it adds up. Young guys don't have as much baggage, because they haven't experienced much of life." I said, then Thatch opened his mouth to speak, but I held up a finger to stop him.

"This lack of experience is refreshing, because all they want is a good time. They haven't been horribly disappointed by a divorce, or a soul-crushing job. And that kept my flings with young men fun and easy. Seriously, I wanted my personal life to be simple because my professional life was incredibly stressful." I'd never put this into words before, and now that I had, I wondered if I'd made the right choices.

"But didn't you ever feel lonely?" Thatch poured more coffee into his mug. "I'm not knocking young gay guys, because I was one myself, many, many moons ago, but what on earth would you have in common? There are few, if any shared life experiences you could talk about."

"Sharing my life was the last thing on my mind." I murmured, feeling a lump form in my throat. My eyes were still glued to the swimming pool. I couldn't look Thatch in the eye, because I was afraid I'd blurt out that maybe, just maybe I was interested in sharing it now.

Then, he cleared his throat and spoke. "In 1982, I woke up on Christmas morning and found an IBM PC under the tree. It was amazing, and that's when I first began writing. Well, when I wasn't playing Atari on this huge, color console TV." Thatch said, and I turned in my seat to face him. Something in his voice compelled me to. "Of course, I barely got any face time with those ancient machines because Daddy wouldn't stop playing with either of them."

I chuckled, remembering my first experiences with computers. "Pop would take me to the office on weekends. While he worked in his private office, I'd fiddle with the computers and xerox machines where his secretaries worked." A juvenile grin stretched across my face. "Can't believe I'm telling you this, but I used to xerox my ass and leave copies in random desks."

Thatch guffawed, and clapped his hands. "I'd expect nothing less from you."

"Then Pop bought me an Apple, what did they call them

back then?" I drummed my fingers on the table. "Oh, it was an Apple Macintosh 128K. Now that was a fun little machine. But looking back on it, they really didn't do too terribly much, but damn, I felt so cool having one of my very own, though I spent more time in front of the boob tube. My favorite shows were on PBS, mostly British comedies like Are You Being Served."

"I used to watch that!" Thatch smacked his knee. "That crazy woman with the constantly changing hair color. Damn it, what was her name again?"

"Mrs. Slocombe." I threw my head back and laughed. "Her poor pussy was always giving her problems. Gosh, I haven't thought of this stuff in ages."

"When did you figure out you were gay?" Thatch asked, his voice deepening.

"Huh." I placed my finger on my chin and thought for a moment. "It was when I was very young, maybe when I was eight? I'd come home from school and the nanny always wanted to watch television. In the afternoons they showed reruns of popular shows from the 60s and 70s. My favorite was Hogan's Heroes."

"I remember that one." Thatch said.

"Well, my very first crush was the character of Colonel Hogan, and if I recall correctly, the actor's name was Robert Crane. There was some sort of sex scandal about him. Anyhow, I never crushed on girls, but I'd dream about being one of Hogan's Heroes every single night. We'd sneak out of the prison camp together and bomb the Germans." I shut my eyes for a moment, remembering how innocent I was back then.

"My first boy crush was also a TV character. Brock Reynolds, from The Young and The Restless. That man was so hot. He had a dimple in his chin, thick brown hair, and his mother was such a diva. Her name was Kay Chancellor."

"This trip down memory lane has been fun, but why are we

doing it?" I asked, then poured the rest of the coffee into my cup.

"Have you ever been able to have a similar conversation with a twenty-something?" Thatch winked.

I shook my head no.

"They have no idea how different our lives were back then. No internet, only three or four television stations to choose from, and TV shows back in the day had actual plots and characters. Not stupid reality shows featuring wealthy housewives with plastic surgery addictions." Thatch laced his hands behind his head and sighed. "Life was simpler, mostly because we weren't glued to our phones."

"I was glued to the telephone attached to the wall in our kitchen." I recalled. "Next to the phone was our pantry, and I'd call up friends and talk for hours in there."

"Honestly, I don't think I'd be a writer today if we'd had the internet growing up. Instead of hanging out at the library or watching TV shows with actual characters and plots, I'd have been mindlessly scrolling and playing games on a stupid phone." Thatch said.

"One of the happiest days of my life was finding a pile of gay porn magazines in the parking deck across from Dad's office building." I grinned. "They were just lying on the ground by the passenger side of his car. I stashed them in my bookbag before Dad found them. When I got home I went straight to my room and beat my dick like it owed me money. Ah, the good old days. Actual porn magazines, and video tapes."

We both sighed. Thatch glanced over to me, catching my eye. He started to speak, then stopped.

"What were you going to say?"I murmured.

"Why did you really move down south, Cary?"

"I spent my entire professional life racing around trying to make as much money as possible, and it was exhausting.

Retirement is out of the question, but I want to slow down and enjoy the last half of my life." I felt tears building up, so I bit my lip to distract myself. "Thing is, I don't like dwelling on the past." My voice trembled, and I fought to keep it steady. "I've always kept my sights on the future, but I must admit, it is kind of nice hanging around you, because you understand the world that shaped me. Shaped our entire generation." I said, my brain now thoroughly wrapped in memories.

"Yeah. I think that's why I've never dated younger men. They don't understand where I'm coming from half the time." Thatch abruptly got to his feet. "I've got to get ready," He frowned.

Damn it. His fucking date.

Thatch glanced down at me. "Joey's far too young for me. We're just two guys going to enjoy some live music." He muttered, then placed the remnants of our breakfast on the tray.

"Give Joey a chance. You don't have to marry the guy, just enjoy your time together." I didn't look at him, keeping my eyes firmly on the pool. This was so fucking difficult, me pushing the two of them into each other's arms, but I wasn't ready for anything more than learning to live again, in this older body that had betrayed me. Thatch still had a life to live, and I didn't want to hold him back.

He cleared his throat, and then I heard footsteps walking away. When I turned around in my seat, he was closing the patio door behind him.

———

I didn't go inside for another hour, and when I did, Thatch was nowhere to be found. He was probably in his room getting ready for his date with Joey.

It took about five minutes to make it up the stairs, but I did it all on my own, and didn't have to stop and rest once. When I got to the top of the stairs, Thatch's bedroom door was shut. I stared at it for a long time, my feet unable to move. My fingers gently swiped across the doorknob, wanting to open it and see that handsome man up close. I remembered vividly his gorgeous body, those long, lean limbs, and glistening skin. His wavy hair brushing over his bare shoulders.

"What the hell is wrong with me? Now I'm getting turned on by gray hair. I've gotta get out of this house soon or I'm going to lose my mind." I whispered, shaking my head.

When I heard footsteps on the other side of the door, my feet finally began to work. I turned the corner and was standing in front of my room, then the doorbell rang. Moments later, I heard the door to Thatch's room open, then feet trudging down the stairs. I quietly opened my door, then walked to the window and pulled the curtain to the side.

I couldn't hear what they were saying as they left the house and got into Joey's car, but I did see the kiss he planted on Thatch's cheek.

After they were out of sight, I crawled into bed and pulled the covers over my head.

"Why now?" I smacked the mattress with the palm of my hand. "I've avoided messy, emotional shit my entire life. So why am I feeling like this about Thatch?"

CHAPTER 18

THATCH

" was kind of expecting the concerts to be outside on the grounds, not inside one of the event halls." Joey said as we took our seats.

The Bluegrass festival reminded me of the book conventions I'd attended over the years, except there was live music on stage. There were only a few hundred people in attendance, and we had excellent seats near the front. The first band was tuning their instruments and ignoring the crowd, who were still claiming their seats.

"Excuse me." An older woman spoke, and we turned our heads in her direction. Her blonde hair was in a beehive, and she wore neon-colored plastic bracelets and necklaces I hadn't seen since the 80s. "Would you and your son mind letting me through? My seat is in the center of the row."

It took me a second to understand what she'd just said. I got to my feet, and Joey did the same. As she passed, I could smell her fragrance. It was what my grandmother had worn, I was sure of it.

"Sorry about that." Joey muttered as we settled back into our seats.

"Sorry about what?"

"You know what she said about me being your son." He huffed. "She was just assuming…"

"A logical assumption, in my opinion." I grinned and patted him on the knee. "We kind of resemble each other. Both of us have longer hair, except mine is salt and pepper, and yours is brown. Even our face shapes are similar, both oval. She's from a different generation, and the first thing that popped into her mind was that we were related. Don't take it personally. I don't."

"Whatever," Joey grumbled, then whispered in my ear. "What perfume is she wearing? It smells, well, not awful, but really strong."

"Youth Dew," I giggled. "My grandmother wore it every single day of her life, bless her heart. When she was young, it was very popular."

"It smells like motor oil mixed with flowers." Joey winked.

"Hush, she might hear us." I whispered, then the lights darkened overhead, and they announced the first band. I felt something on my lap, and to my surprise, Joey's hand found mine and covered it. My first reaction was to pull my hand away. Besides Brian and Sam, nobody had held my hand in decades, but this was a date, so I had to expect it.

The sound of a fiddle filled the room, and the audience fell silent. I snuck a glance in Joey's direction. His gaze was trained on the stage, his mouth ajar. He had thin lips, a hooked nose, and the beginnings of crow's feet. In ten more years, he'd hit maximum attractiveness. I'd always thought men were at their best when they hit forty. From there it wasn't downhill, more like a softening as their faces aged.

"Hey, are you going to stare at me, or watch the show?" Joey whispered, and squeezed my hand.

"Sorry."

"I'm glad you came to the festival with me." Joey smiled. "Have you ever been to O'Henry's before?"

After a few hours of bluegrass, Joey suggested we go to the local gay bar. "No. I've lived in Asheville for years, but haven't had the chance to come here." I scanned the room full of men and felt out of place. It was Saturday night, and it was filled with younger guys. They were all wearing skimpy clothing and had hair colors not found in nature. I also noticed quite a few drag queens milling around.

"You'll find me here most Saturday nights," Joey said. "They have two drag shows, and it can get pretty rowdy."

We were seated at a table next to a stage, and I tried to remember the last time I'd seen a drag show. "This is the first drag show I've been to in..." I drummed my fingers on the table. "...wow, since before Sam was born, so almost twenty-five years."

"You've got a lot of catching up to do." Joey reached across the table and placed his hand on mine. "I love watching the performers. The makeup, the lights, and the fierce attitude. There's no better way to spend a Saturday night."

"Well, it was difficult for Brian and I to go anywhere since we had Sam. When he was young, we mostly went to kids' movies, or on play dates with his little friends." I smiled, remembering those days. Having Sam was the most important event of my life, and I hadn't missed gay bars one single bit. "Watching Sam grow up was such a gift. We didn't have time to party, but we still had fun."

"Well, maybe it's time to rejoin the living, and live a little." Joey stood up. "I'm going to the bar for a drink. What are you having?"

I wanted a cup of tea, but according to Joey, I needed to live a little. "Whatever you're having is great."

I watched him snake through the crowd, and realized I didn't miss coming to these types of places. They were a blast when I was single, and in my twenties, but now I felt disconnected from everyone around me. Anyway, what the hell did he mean by rejoining the living? As far as I was concerned, I'd lived a very full life so far, and going to bars just hadn't been important to me then, and apparently now.

I didn't want to rain on Joey's parade, but after two drinks, I felt like insisting he take me home. A ball of resentment was churning in my stomach, because I'd lived a helluva lot, and didn't regret a single moment. That was what I hated the most about aging, the assumption that you didn't have fun anymore, but I'd play the part of the attentive date like I was expected to. As far as I was concerned, Joey and I could be friends, but I didn't see a future for us beyond that.

———

"I had a great time with you, Thatch." Joey murmured when the security gate opened on my driveway. "Are you okay? Because, you've been awfully quiet."

My resentment was long gone. Joey was thirty-one, exactly twenty years younger than me, and was acting like a thirty-one-year-old single guy. There was absolutely nothing wrong with him, and if I was his age and had never had Sam, most likely I would've had a great time with him.

"Joey, I had a wonderful time with you tonight..."

"But..." Joey said, his voice dropping.

"...I think we are better off as friends." I stared at his face while he drove toward the house. His jaw clenched so hard I hoped he didn't crack it. "You may not think so, and I'm sorry, but..." Shit, why the hell did I feel the urge to explain myself? "...it would be for the best..."

Joey's shoulders slumped as he parked in front of my door. "I figured this would happen. A successful guy like you doesn't fall for dudes like me." He muttered, then the doors unlocked with a loud click. "Is it because of my..."

"Don't." I held my hand up. "I genuinely like you, and think you're fun to hang out with, but I just don't see us ever evolving beyond what we have already."

"You're an incredibly sexy man, Thatch." Joey murmured, and I felt heat rising up my neck. "Can we just keep this open-ended, instead of ending it entirely, because I swear if you give me a chance you won't regret it."

Since nobody had told me I was sexy in years, my resolve faltered. "Well, sure." I sighed. "You're right. I shouldn't be such an absolutist about everything. Even Cary has told me to lighten up."

"Can I kiss you goodnight?" Joey's eyes widened, and even in the dim light of the car, I could see his cheeks blush. I hadn't been kissed in such a long time.

I nodded, and Joey's face came closer to mine. He placed his hand behind my neck, and his fingers were warm. My eyes shut, and I was nervous he would go tongue diving in my mouth. Instead, he brushed his lips across mine and pulled back.

"Goodnight, and thanks for spending a great day with me, Thatch." He said, his eyes locked on mine.

"Goodnight," I breathed, then stepped out of the car and shut the door.

Moments later, I watched his red taillights fade away as he

drove towards the main road, then a strange feeling hit me, like I was being watched. I glanced up and saw Cary staring out the window. He waggled his fingers at me, and a smile split my face.

To my surprise, Cary was on his way down the steps as soon as I shut the front door.

"So, how was your date with Joey?" He called down, and suddenly I was at a loss for words.

CHAPTER 19

CARY

Thatch mumbled something I couldn't quite hear. I was halfway down the steps, and it surprised me how fast I was moving. Instead of my usual clutching the railing and praying I didn't tumble to the bottom, I was descending the stairs like an almost normal person.

"I couldn't hear you." I said when I reached the bottom, slightly out of breath.

"It was, um, interesting." Thatch grinned. "What are you still doing up?"

Sleep and I were hardly friends, and knowing Cary was out with Joey made it even more difficult to drift off, but there was no way in hell I was telling Thatch about it.

"I don't sleep much. It's rare for me to get over four or five hours a night." I replied.

"Me too." Thatch said with his huge, toothy grin. Come to think of it, I had a similar smile splitting my face. "Are you hungry?"

"Always, especially when it's something you've made. You are one of the best cooks I've ever met." I patted Thatch on the shoulder, and I noticed Thatch's posture relaxing, and a slight flush inched up his neck.

"No, I'm not. You are falling in love with southern food, and I happen to be decent at making it. Let's see what's in the fridge." Thatch reached out his hand, hesitated, then spun around and strolled into the kitchen.

I followed behind him, and it struck me that we had a strange awkwardness between us that I'd never felt with anyone else before. It was like there was something unsaid that needed to be spoken. I knew what I wanted to say, but was unsure of Thatch's reaction.

"Sit." Thatch said, and I sat in my usual place by the counter. "What time is it?"

I pulled my phone out of my pocket. "Almost midnight. You must have had fun if you stayed out this late." I was fishing for information about his date, but didn't want to seem too obvious about it. Then my phone pinged. I glanced at the screen and saw a message from Sam.

I'm almost at Dad's house

"Your fabulous son just texted me. He says he'll be here any minute." I slid the phone back into the pocket of my robe.

"Why on earth is Sam coming here so late?" Thatch said, and started taking food out of the fridge. "Might as well make a full meal. I'm starving, and Sam is always hungry. Did you invite him?"

"No. I haven't spoken to him in days." I replied, wondering why he was coming here too.

"Are you handy with a knife?" Thatch asked, and when I nodded yes, he pulled a bowl of round green things out of the fridge and set them in front of me. Next to the bowl, he placed a well-used wooden cutting board, then pulled a knife out of the block and handed it to me.

"What are these things?" I pointed at the bowl. "They look like tomatoes, but they're green."

"That's because I'm making fried green tomatoes. Hope you don't mind a little stink, but I've got some fish that needs to be eaten, so I'll fry that up as well." Thatch said, then froze. "Shoot, I'm not sure you should eat all this fried stuff."

"I'm feeling better, I promise. Remember, it wasn't my heart giving me trouble."

"Yes, but Joey told me…"

"Speaking of Joey, how was your date?" I interrupted. Not only did I want to pump him for information, the idea of fried green tomatoes intrigued me. I loved that movie with Kathy Bates.

Thatch shrugged. "It was okay, I guess."

Huh. Just okay? My stomach fluttered. "Oh, so what did the two of you do again? I remember you saying something about hillbilly music."

Thatch winked at me, and muttered, "Hillbilly music." He turned back to the fridge and began pulling out all sorts of stuff. "It was a bluegrass festival, and I enjoyed the music." He shut the refrigerator door, then turned and gripped the counter. "After the concert, he took me to a gay bar. Hadn't been to one in years."

"You hated it. I can tell." I grinned and bit my lower lip. There was no way in hell Thatch would enjoy hanging out in bars. He was too set in his ways.

"I didn't hate it," Thatch smiled, then positioned himself beside me and grabbed the knife and a tomato. "Start earning your keep, Cary." He handed them to me, then he walked behind me and I felt his hand grip my shoulder.

"Do you ever miss being married? Because I bet you were an excellent husband." I asked, and Thatch let go of my shoulder and sat on the stool next to me.

"Yes, but I don't miss being married to Brian." He grabbed a large bowl that had a bag and a sifter in it, then began measuring flour into a cup.

"Why? Didn't you two have a lot in common? I mean, he is your literary agent." I carefully laid the edge of the knife against the green tomato and cut into it.

"Well, we did have a lot in common, but mostly, that was Sam. Once he left for college, there wasn't much beyond my writing career holding us together. Also, he became really grumpy towards the end." Thatch sighed, wiping his hands on a towel. Then he began sifting the flour, which had an odd metal whooshing sound to it. "I think he was sleeping around on me too, but he's never 'fessed up. Seriously, the only time I miss being married is in the evening, when I'm all alone in my bed."

"Why only at night?"

"Well, it's the being alone bit that can be rough, though I'm used to it now. After Brian left, I used to hug my pillow when trying to sleep. Now I kind of like having the entire bed to myself. I get in the middle of it, and wrap the blankets around me like a cocoon." Thatch finished sifting the flour, then added salt and pepper to it, along with some red powder.

"What's that stuff?" I pointed at it.

"Paprika. It's my secret ingredient, and I've never told anyone that I use it." Thatch grinned, and placed his arm over my shoulder, and my mouth went dry. "Don't tell anyone."

The door that led to the garage suddenly flew open and Sam strolled in with a big grin on his face. I jumped, and Thatch yanked his arm from my shoulder and rose to his feet.

"Hi Dad, Cary." Sam said, and he swung his backpack off of his shoulder and placed it on one of the stools. Then he stood there, just staring at us. "Did I come in at a bad time?"

"No, no, of course not." Thatch mumbled, staring at the floor. "Why are you here?"

"That's hardly the thing to say to your favorite child." Sam grinned, then walked over to Thatch and gave him a quick hug.

"You're his only kid. He's gotta love you." I stated dryly, and to my surprise, Sam pecked me on the forehead.

"Why do I have the feeling that I caught you two doing something bad?" Sam's eyebrows rose toward the ceiling.

I glanced over at Thatch, and we both shrugged our shoulders at the same time.

"Well, I'm here because Dad stood me up." Sam sat on the other side of me, grabbed the cutting board and knife, and began slicing up the tomatoes much faster than I could.

"What do you mean, Brian stood you up?" Thatch sat back down and began stirring the flour mix. "Isn't he in New York?"

"He asked me to meet him at the house in Nags Head, but at the last minute, he canceled. So I had to figure out what to do this weekend. The guys at school wanted to go to Raleigh and check out some new clubs on Glenwood South, but I decided to come here to see how you guys are getting along." Sam put down the knife, the tomatoes all sliced. "And from what I see, you guys are doing great. Oh, I'll sleep in the guest room, Cary. You don't have to change rooms because of me. I thought you guys would be asleep by now."

"I don't sleep much, and neither does your Dad," I grinned at Thatch, who matched my grin with one of his own. "Guess where Thatch was earlier this evening?"

"Cary, don't..." Thatch began, but Sam cut him off.

"Let me guess. The library? Or did you make a trip to the gourmet market?"

"He was at a gay bar." I stated, and Thatch frowned. Shit, maybe I shouldn't have mentioned it.

"You've got to be kidding me. I don't think Dad's seen the

inside of a gay bar since before I was born." Sam said, then got off the stool, went to the fridge and pulled a beer out.

"It was extra boring, for your information." Thatch commented, then put his face in his hands and groaned. "I won't be going out with Joey again."

"Wait, do you mean that hot nurse from the hospital?" Sam tilted his head, his eyes squishing together. "Isn't he kind of young for you?"

Thatch smacked the counter, and both Sam and I jumped. "Why is it okay for you to date older men like Cary, and for Brian to date guys your age, but if I go out with someone younger, everyone gets bent out of shape?"

"Dad, I'm sorry, and I wasn't upset or anything. It's just I can't picture you enjoying being out with a younger guy." Sam twisted off the top of his beer and a little of it foamed onto his fingers, which he licked clean. Thatch ripped off a paper towel and handed it to him.

"Mind your manners in front of company." Thatch sighed. "Honestly, I felt nothing for Joey beyond, I don't know, grati- tude for the ego strokes." He placed his arm over my shoulder, turned to me, and smiled. "I can't believe I'm admitting this, but I'm having a lot more fun with this guy." He poked me in the ribs, and to my surprise, I giggled.

Sam looked me in the eye, then his gaze shifted to Thatch. He placed his beer down, grabbed a ripe tomato out of a bowl in the middle of the counter, and bit into it. Thatch handed him another paper towel. Once he was finished eating, he wiped his hands off, and turned to Thatch.

"Dad, I need to talk to you about something..." He tilted his head in the direction of the living room. "Alone."

CHAPTER 20
THATCH

"I don't want to leave Cary here all by himself." I said, wondering why Sam needed to speak to me alone. "He's not a cook, and this food won't fix itself."

Sam's brow furrowed. "Dad, Cary will be fine for five minutes, won't you?" He nodded at Cary, who shrugged.

"Sure, you two go do your family thing. I'll, um, cut something up?" He stared at the counter in front of him.

"Fine. Go to the guest room, and I'll meet you there in a moment." I frowned, then turned to Cary. "Do you know how to peel potatoes?"

He nodded, so I went to the pantry and pulled out a few potatoes. After placing them in front of him with a peeler, I left the kitchen.

What on earth could Sam want? Was he in trouble at school? Or had Brian done more than stand him up? I took the steps two at a time, and when I got to the guest room, the door was wide open. Sam was perched on a corner of the bed, a cheshire cat grin plastered to his face.

"So, what are you so desperate to talk to me about?"

"I've met someone." Sam winked. "He's super cute, and only a couple of years older than me."

"Okay. You've met someone. That's great, Sam. But you didn't ask to speak to me alone just because of that, unless you were nervous about upsetting Cary." I crossed my arms over my chest, curious to discover the real reason Sam wanted us to speak in private.

"Dad, Cary wouldn't be upset about me dating anyone. Trust me. We never had a serious relationship in the first place. Plus..." Sam stood up and placed his hands on my shoulders. "Cary has never looked at me the way he looks at you."

"What?" I sank down onto the bed, and Sam began pacing around the room.

"Dad, you and Cary have some serious chemistry going on. Like, it was obvious from the moment I stepped into the kitchen. It was kind of icky, to be honest, like the time I walked in on you and my other..."

"Wait, wait, wait." I held my hands up. "Cary is only into young guys, and I'm older than he is. Even if he was interested in me, I'd..."

"He is. Dad, If you are worried that I'll be upset with you dating Cary, you're wrong. Hell. we never did anything more than fool around, if you know what I mean. In fact, I think it's the best thing ever. You two are perfect for each other." Sam sat next to me. "You must admit, Cary is very charming, charismatic even. And he matches you when it comes to intellect, and that's hard to do."

"It's unnerving, to be honest. One minute he comes across as the most shallow man in the universe, and the next he's practically reading my mind." My heart was pounding in my chest, because I wanted to believe what Sam was saying. When I arrived home after my lackluster date with Joey, I'd been so damned happy to see Cary. Being around him was easy, while being with Joey had left me feeling empty, and old.

"Maybe you've got a point." I murmured. "But I doubt Cary sees it the same way. In his eyes, I'm just a nurse or something. It's not like he wanted to stay here."

"Dad, what's the worst thing that could happen? He says he's not interested, and you move on. He's looking much healthier than the last time I saw him, so it's not like he's going to be here much longer. This might be your only chance to see what could happen between the two of you. And honestly, if I ever wanted a stepdad, I'd want it to be him." Sam stood up. "C'mon, let's go back to the kitchen before Cary decides to cook and burns the house down."

———

"...and Jenny has this strange habit of sleeping with people I do business with, and it's not just men. I asked her why she did this once, and she was startlingly honest about it. Said it made her feel powerful." Cary shook his head and smiled. "That and she's a self-proclaimed nymphomaniac who kick-starts her vibrator if she goes longer than a couple of days without any action. Oh, and she has excellent taste." Cary leered at me. Well, I think he was leering. "She thinks your dad is hot." He said this to Sam, who winked at me.

I blushed, then raised my beer. "To Jenny. A woman who owns her sexuality and enjoys it."

The three of us sipped our beers and Sam yawned. "Guys, it's almost four in the morning. I'm going to bed." He drained the rest of his beer, belched, and got to his feet, clutching the kitchen counter to keep steady. "Don't do anything I wouldn't do."

"That leaves us with too many options, young man." Cary

said, but his eyes never left mine. God, I hope Sam was right about Cary, because there was something between us. I'd swear on it. But the odds of me meeting a man my age who found me attractive were slim.

Sam staggered out of the kitchen, and when I heard his feet on the stairs, Cary laid his hand on top of mine. I froze, and the skin on my arms pebbled at his touch.

"Your son was never in love with me, and I don't want you to—"

"I know," I murmured, and felt a lump forming in my throat. "When we went upstairs to talk, he was trying to set us up." I waved my other hand between us. "Sam thinks we have chemistry or something."

"Do we?"

My mouth went dry, and I desperately wanted to change the conversation. I was attracted to him, but it had been so long since I'd had these sorts of feelings that I felt paralyzed.

"Maybe." I murmured, and I turned the hand Cary was covering over, and our fingers entwined.

"I can feel your pulse." Cary said, his eyes boring into mine. "My pulse is racing too. It's late, Thatch, and after drinking and talking most of the night, perhaps we should resume this conversation after we've both had a good night's sleep."

I inhaled deeply and felt conflicted. Taking things slowly was the logical way of proceeding, but I wasn't feeling particularly patient.

"Hey, I'll be honest with you, Thatch. I'm wiped out, and you'll probably have to help me up the stairs. I am feeling something for you, but, I'm, well, unsure, because I've never had these kinds of feelings before. All my life I've acted impulsively, and I've made some pretty sketchy decisions because of it." Cary brought my hand up to his mouth and kissed it. "Having a near-death experience changes how you see the world. I need rest, and I need to make sure I'm doing the right thing. You have your family and friends, and all I have is Jenny and people I pay to do stuff for me. I need a little time."

God, I wanted to grab him by the shoulders and kiss him the way I'd longed to be kissed for so long now. Years of loneliness weighed heavily on my shoulders, and I realized Cary was right. When we were young, our bodies often would act before our brains could even process our desires. Now we had the gift of time and control. Making the right decisions was more important than doing something we might both regret.

"Let's get you to bed." I murmured, and Cary let go of my hand and pushed himself up, holding on to the counter for support. He trudged ahead of me, and when we got to the stairs, he turned toward me. I wrapped my arm around him, and he did the same to me.

"Do you have a thing for sick guys?" Cary murmured as we started up the steps.

"No, trust me. After nursing Sam through all his childhood illnesses, I have no desire to be anyone's nursemaid." I said, and Cary let go of me.

"I have to do this kind of stuff myself, if I'm ever going to get better." He said, gripping the railing.

"Are you sure?" I asked, missing his arm around my waist.

"The next time you put your arms around me, it won't be because I can't move around by myself." Cary said, then surprised me by walking steadily up the stairs with only the railing for support. I followed a foot behind him in case he needed help. When he got to the top of the staircase, he turned around and grinned.

"See, I can do it!" He laughed. "God, I hate feeling helpless."

"You can do anything you set your mind to. That's why you are such a success." I grinned back at him. A few feet later we were in front of my bedroom. Cary stared me in the eye, then glanced into my open door.

"Goodnight," He murmured, his smile flatlining, then he shook his head a few times, and I wondered what he was thinking.

I closed the gap between us, wrapped my arms around his waist and brushed my lips across his. His body trembled, and when I pulled him in for a tight hug, I could feel his heart thumping hard against mine. Then I let go of him and walked through my door. When I turned to shut it, he was slowly turning around.

"Don't think too much, or too long, Cary." I whispered, and shut the door.

CHAPTER 21

CARY

"Damn it," I groaned, rubbing my eyes. I'd forgotten to shut the drapes before getting into bed, and now the bright, early morning rays were blinding me. I got to my feet, yawned, then shut them and climbed back into bed. That's when I realized something else was startling me.

"Well, hello, old friend." I squeezed my morning wood. "Long time since you were up, so to speak."

I lay there, wondering if I had to piss, or if it was a genuine erection, then my eyes fluttered shut, and a vision of Thatch in his lean, naked glory filled my head. My muscles relaxed, then I gripped my cock at the base and slowly moved my hand up and down my shaft.

"What would a genuine kiss taste like?" I whispered, and in my imagination felt Thatch's arms tightening around me, and his lips moving forward until they crashed into mine. My mouth grew wetter, imagining Thatch's tongue dancing with mine, and I reached down with my other hand, squeezed my balls, and groaned.

Suddenly I could smell him, his old-fashioned manly scent

filling my nostrils. My hand tightened around my length, and I felt the beginning of an orgasm approach. It had been quite awhile since I'd last come, and I knew I wouldn't be able to last for long, especially when I imagined his thick...

A car horn interrupted me. "What the actual fuck is going on?"

I went to the window and pulled the drapes back a couple of inches. Whoever it was couldn't know that the three of us had been up late drinking and talking. Plus, they had to know the security code for the gate. A bleached-blonde head emerged from the driver's side window of an SUV. It was a woman, and when she glanced up to the house, I shut the drapes, then I heard what sounded like the garage doors opening.

"Celia Mae." I sighed, not knowing what I thought of Thatch's sister. While she'd never been rude to me, she had skirted the border between civility and hostility in every one of our interactions. Knowing she probably had a key, I threw on my robe to give Thatch the news that his sister was here.

"Wait." I realized I was naked under the robe. "My pajamas, too. Strange things happen when this family is all together, and I'd better not leave anything to chance."

Less than a minute passed before I was standing in front of Thatch's door, my fist ready to knock.

"Thatch?" I heard Celia Mae's voice calling from down-stairs. "Thatch? I've got the funniest thing to show you!"

I didn't know what time it was, but from the bit of daylight I'd seen, it had to be mid-morning. Did she get up at the crack of dawn to drive here from wherever she lived? I raised my fist to knock on the door again and then it flew open, revealing Thatch in a skin-tight black t-shirt and gray sweats.

"Oh, my God!" We said at the same time, and then Thatch combed his fingers through his gorgeous silver hair and smiled.

"Hey, you." Thatch opened his arms and without thought, I

walked into them.

"Oh, my God, you smell just like I dreamed you would." I murmured, and his arms tightened around my waist.

"You've been dreaming about me, huh?" He whispered in my ear, and I felt my morning wood returning.

"What the hell is he still doing here?" Celia Mae's voice trilled from behind us.

"Shit." I muttered, then Thatch gently pushed me back, and I turned around to face his sister. I took a deep breath, forced a smile on my face, and said, "What a pleasure it is to see you again."

"Yeah, right." She said, then I noticed a twinkle in her eye. "Did I, um, interrupt something?"

Thatch coughed, and I felt blood racing to my cheeks.

"I saw Sam's car in the garage. What did ya'll do? Throw a party and forget to invite me?" She strolled past us down the hallway and turned a corner. Moments later, we heard Sam scream, "Oh shit!" Then Celia Mae cackled and told him to get his ass out of bed.

"Let me put on a robe and we can see what my sister wants." Thatch yawned, stretching his hands over his head, then he cocked his head to the side. "A kiss good morning?"

"If you don't mind morning breath."

"A peck will do." Thatch leaned into me, then froze. Celia Mae had to be standing behind us.

"Well, what are you waiting for, big brother? Kiss the fool." She drawled, and Thatch's lips twisted into a smile. "Go on, I got important stuff to tell ya."

Thatch brushed his lips over mine, backed into his bedroom, then shut the door. "I'll be downstairs in a minute. Go on without me." His muffled voice said. "Celia Mae, start some breakfast."

I spun around, and Celia Mae hugged me. My arms

remained stiff by my sides, then she muttered, "I don't know how you did it, but damn, it's been a long time since my brother looked happy." She stepped back, her arms holding my elbows. "You look a helluva lot better, Cary. C'mon, help me whip up some breakfast."

She apparently thought I was going to run away, or that I needed help down the stairs, because she kept a firm grip on my elbow all the way to the kitchen.

When we got there, I noticed an array of books and papers on the counter that hadn't been there before. "What's all this?" I gestured toward the stuff, and she let go of me.

"Sit, I know you can't cook. I'll get some coffee started and when the boys get down here, I'll tell you all about it." She said, and I noticed her struggling not to laugh. "But, I'll tell you this much. Women lived with some fucked-up shit until recently."

I shrugged my shoulders and sat down. A moment later Sam trudged into the room, his eyes bloodshot and the faint scent of alcohol was seeping from his pores. Last night he'd drunk far more beer than Thatch and me, thinking he could sleep in before driving back to Chapel Hill.

"Morning." He mumbled, then sat on the stool next to me and laid his head on my shoulder. "Why am I not asleep?"

Celia Mae opened the pantry and eyed it, then she walked inside and came back out with a couple of empty beer bottles she must have pulled from the recycling bin. "Did y'all have a party last night?" She clinked them together. "How rude of you not to invite me."

"It was a spur-of-the-moment thing, promise." I said, then Thatch came in and sat on the other side of me.

"Can I have your other shoulder?" He winked, and rested his head on it for a moment, then kissed me on the cheek. I would swear every time he kissed me I could feel my cock twitch, and this was not the time or place for that. And since

Thatch's sister had unexpectedly arrived, I wondered if we'd ever have time to figure out what was happening between us.

"Here," Celia Mae poured each of us a cup of coffee and set them down in front of us. "Start drinking that, because you need to be awake to hear what I've discovered."

Thatch pulled his phone out of his robe's pocket. "Celia Mae, are you aware that it's only ten in the morning?"

"Aww, did you three stay up late partying?" She placed a hand on her hip and winked. "You're a bad influence on my boys, Cary. Before they met you, they did nothing fun. Hell, you know what? I'm going to make myself a Bloody Mary." She clapped her hands and laughed. "Time to start day drinking!"

Sam moaned in my ear, and I put an arm around his shoulders to keep him upright.

"Durham is three-and-a-half hours from here. Why on earth did you get up so early?" Thatch asked and yawned again.

"Because, I was at Cousin Joe's house in Hickory last night. That's practically around the corner." Celia Mae pulled a bottle of vodka from the freezer, then got a bottle of Bloody Mary mix from the fridge. "We had a little party too, but we can handle our liquor better than y'all."

"What is so exciting you had to stop by and share it?" Thatch asked, and Celia Mae pointed at him, then the vodka. He swallowed, then shook his head no.

"You see that manila envelope, Cary?" She asked. I nodded. "Open it."

I did as instructed while she broke off a stalk of celery and placed it in her glass. An old book fell out, with several yellowing documents.

"Those are Granny Floris's things. Her diary, and, well, some bizarre archaic shit they put her through when she was only a teenager." Celia Mae sipped her drink, then placed it on the counter and poured more vodka in it.

"Why does Joe have this stuff?" Thatch asked.

"Because, he's a straight guy who loves the bible, just like she did." Celia Mae said, then spoke to me. "My granny was a very religious woman who disapproved of Thatch quite loudly. I don't think Sam even met her, and she only lived about an hour away. It was a shame, because she never got to meet the brilliant alcoholic he's become."

"Shut up, Aunt Celia Mae." Sam muttered, then lifted his head from my shoulder. "I met her once." He leaned over, so he could see Thatch. "My birth Mom took me to a family reunion." He glanced up to Celia Mae. "Granny told me Dad was evil, and that I should get away from him as soon as possible. I was only twelve years old, I think."

"Jesus," Thatch's voice trembled. "She was the evil one, not me. So, you know my history with Granny. Why are you showing me this stuff?" He gestured toward the counter, now littered with papers and books.

"Her life was, let's just put it this way, bizarre. I placed a paper clip where I want you to read in her diary." She drained her drink and pointed at Thatch. "Go on, read it."

He picked up the book, opened it, and scanned the page. His eyes widened. "This can't be real."

"It is." Celia Mae slid an old yellow piece of paper in front of Thatch. "Here's the proof."

He scanned the page, then his mouth fell open. "Oh. My. God."

"May I?" I asked Celia Mae. She smirked and nodded. I carefully picked it up and began to read.

In large script at the top of the page, it stated what it was.

Certificate of Virginity

Underneath that was a notary's seal.

To whom it may concern. Floris Ann Beaumont has never been touched in an impure fashion. Her hymen was breached during a medical procedure.

Dr. Thornton B. Smith signed it.

"You've got to be kidding." I muttered, and Sam took the certificate from me. "But, why?"

"It says here in her diary that she was suffering from bad cramps, and her grandmother took her to see this quack. He had to remove her hymen in order to perform an exam. Afterwards he gave her the certificate to show her future husband." Thatch chuckled. "Wow, times were very different in the 1940s."

"If that had happened to me, I would've gone whoring it up." Celia Mae grinned. "Hell, I could sleep with anyone I wanted, then show my future hubby that I was still pure."

"I'm a virgin." Sam grinned at us, and we all gaped at him. "What? I've never been with a woman, so in that regard I'm still pure. I wonder if I could get a certificate like this?"

"To show who?" Celia Mae crunched down on her celery stalk. "Trust me, nobody will believe it."

"I don't know. I think I'd frame it or something, just for laughs." Sam said, then pointed at his aunt. "Would you make me a bloody too? Hair of the Dog is the only cure for my hangover now."

Something buzzed against my thigh and I realized it was my phone. I pulled it out and there was a message from Dr. Creighton.

Joey Davies says you are on the mend

I will stop by tomorrow afternoon at three and see if you're okay to travel

My stomach clenched, and it was suddenly hard to breathe. I didn't want to leave. Not yet.

"What's wrong, Cary?" Celia Mae arched an eyebrow. "You look like someone kicked your dog."

CHAPTER 22

THATCH

Cary laid his phone on the counter and sighed. "Dr. Creighton and Joey are stopping by tomorrow afternoon. Joey wants me out of... sorry, I mean, he thinks I'm healthy enough to travel."

I knew what he wanted to say. Joey was a great guy, but it wouldn't surprise me in the least if he wanted Cary to hit the road. The problem was that I wasn't sure whether I wanted him to leave. There were unspoken words between us, and with Sam and Celia Mae here, there weren't many opportunities for us to say them.

"Aunt Celia Mae, skip the Bloody Mary. I'm going back to bed." Sam slowly got to his feet, clutching the counter.

"Well, I'm sure your liver will thank you." Cary remarked with a grin. "Are you sure you don't want to eat? You'll feel better if you do."

Sam groaned and sat back down. "I have to be back in Chapel Hill tonight, because I teach an early morning class. If I don't sleep, at least another couple of hours, I won't be able to drive."

"You are definitely not getting any more booze, Sam, but that's not stopping me from…" Celia Mae glanced in my direction, and I'd swear a light bulb lit up over her head. "… making us a tasty breakfast, so both of us can hit the highway. I've got to be at work early, too." She picked up the bottle of vodka and put it back in the freezer. "Cary, it's time you learned how to cook. Thatch can teach you how to make his famous salsa, and I'll make southwestern omelets."

I turned to Cary and winked. "I won't make you do more than you, um, want to." As soon as the words slipped out of my mouth, I realized they had a double meaning. Salsa was easy, but whatever was brewing between us wasn't. Cary hadn't been seriously involved with anyone before. I suspected he might be a little antsy about things becoming heavy between us, but I didn't know how to keep things light or simple. What did I really want?

"I want to do everything." Cary murmured, and I felt his leg press against mine. "You tell me what you want, and I'll do my best, since I've never done this, I mean, cooked before."

I turned in my seat and stared into his dark, luminous eyes. His lips parted, then Celia Mae cleared her throat and spoke.

"Breakfast first, gentlemen."

———

"Not bad for a rookie chef," Celia Mae said, swiping up the remnants of her breakfast with the last piece of toast. "The salsa was excellent, Cary. Maybe the next time we see each other, I'll teach you how to make omelets."

"That's too advanced for a beginner." I pushed my plate to the side. "But, I'm sure we can introduce you to hash browns. They're as easy as homemade sin to make."

"I don't even know what that means." Cary's leg pressed against mine again, which he'd been doing throughout breakfast. "What is homemade sin?"

"You know, I'm not quite sure." I reached over and grabbed Cary's empty plate and set it on top of mine. "Just a saying we all grew up with. The way I used it was to infer that it is simple to make. The original definition of…"

"Dad, oh my God, take your geek hat off now." Sam shook his head and winked. "Thanks for the delicious meal. I'm feeling better, so I'm taking a shower and driving back to Chapel Hill."

Cary bit his lower lip, and I'd swear it was to keep himself from smiling.

"One more cup of joe and I'll get out of y'alls hair too." Celia Mae stood up, walked over, and hugged me from behind. "Can I have a few words with you in private?" She murmured and kissed the top of my head.

"I know how to load a dishwasher. You two go talk, and I'll clean up the kitchen." Cary patted my thigh and got to his feet.

"You sure you don't want to wait for me to help?" I tilted my head up to him.

"No, no, no. You've been waiting on me hand and foot since I got here. It's time for me to help more. Now go." I shooed them away with my hands. "Gossip about me with Celia Mae, and by the time you're done, the kitchen will be sparkling clean."

"Smart man, and a mindreader, too." Celia Mae winked, took my hand, and dragged me to the stairs.

"Isn't this kind of rude to Cary?" I whispered, but she shook her head no and began pulling me up the steps. When we got to my bedroom door, she opened it, pushed me inside, and shut it behind her.

"Sit." She pointed at my bed, so I perched on the edge. Celia Mae placed her hands on her hips, blew a lock of hair off her forehead, then stared at me for a long moment.

"Well?" I asked impatiently. "I know it's about Cary, so spit it out."

"What the hell is going on with you?" She began pacing in front of me. "The last time I was here, you couldn't tolerate the man. Now you're acting like a rooster set free in a henhouse."

I opened my mouth to speak, but she held a hand up. "I'm not asking you this because I hate him or anything. Hell, I barely know the man, but I want to make sure you understand what you're getting into... Or whom?" She made a circle with one hand and started poking her finger through it.

"Ha ha." I rolled my eyes. "You're forty-nine going on twelve."

"From what I understand, he's only gone out with young-uns, and that includes your son. What's Sam really thinking about this situation? You know, deep down inside." Celia Mae asked.

"Sam is the one pushing us together, or at least, he seemed to be." I replied, and a cloud of confusion settled over me. "He told me they never had a serious relationship. In fact, Sam seems to think Cary and I would be great together."

"Why?"

"What do you mean, why?" I scratched my head.

"Thatch, why do you think you two would work?" She sat next to me and grabbed my hand.

I turned toward her and chose my words carefully. "Would Cary and I make a great couple? I don't know. But, there's something about him that intrigues me, plus he's a damned good-looking man. I'll admit, I'm nervous about whatever is happening between the two of us. The primary reason is, because he's the first man I've been attracted to since Brian and I called it quits. If I don't take a chance now, I might not have that many opportunities in the future." I let go of her hand and covered my face with both of mine. "I'm getting old, Celia Mae, and I don't want to be alone for the rest of my life."

My sister said nothing for a long moment, and I felt pressure building behind my eyes. Was I considering a relationship with Cary solely to avoid the fact that time was passing me by?

"Thatch, I've been single most of my life out of choice. When I was young, Momma told me to be very choosy about selecting a mate. She had that conversation with you too, I bet."

"Sister, all I want to do is, you know... explore the possibility of there being something between me and Cary, that's all." I stood up and held my hand out for her to take. This conversation needed to end, because it was becoming much more serious than I felt comfortable with. She grasped my hand, and I pulled her up. "I'm not about to propose to him, and trust me, after one failed marriage, I'm much pickier than I used to be."

Celia Mae opened her arms for a hug, and I obliged. "Thatch, just for the record, I want you to know that I approve." Her arms tightened around me. "Cary is delightfully obnoxious, which means he'd fit in with our crazy family. Plus, the man is worth a fortune, so he's not a gold digger. He's also making you smile in a way I haven't seen in years. I want my big brother to be happy, because it wasn't just you who went through your last divorce. It rocked everyone who loves you."

"I'll be careful, promise."

"Sam raced out of here after you two went upstairs." Cary told us as he shut the dishwasher. "Said he'd call both of you later in the week."

Celia Mae crossed her arms over her chest and glanced around the kitchen. "Not bad for a man who's never cleaned before." She walked over to the microwave and snatched up her purse, which was next to it. "Cary, hopefully we'll see each other again soon."

"You want to see me again?" Cary winked, and my sister crossed the room and threw her arms around him, then she whispered something in his ear which I couldn't make out. When she released him from her embrace, she took a deep breath and walked to the door. "Don't do anything I wouldn't do, Thatch."

She walked out before I could think of anything to say.

Cary dipped his head, but kept his eyes on mine.

"So, I guess we're alone now." I mumbled. Fear ripped through me, because up until now my family had been a buffer. Now we had none.

"Yeah, I guess we are." Cary said, and I noticed his eyes were wet. Was he going to cry about something? Or was that desire? This was so confusing, like it would be so easy to just grab his hand and take him to my bed. But, that would be the simple thing to do, and something told me that whatever was going on between us ran deeper than just a tumble in the sheets. Plus, we couldn't just stand here staring at each other all day. I had to say something, anything.

"You know what?" I stammered. "We haven't gone swimming yet, have we? I mean, since you arrived."

Cary turned and glanced out the window at the pool. "I can't remember if I brought my swimsuit or not."

Who the hell needs a swimsuit?

A slow smile spread across my cheeks when I thought of what I wanted to say, but couldn't.

But, since I didn't know where this was leading to, I chose a more polite response.

"Don't bother looking for it. You can probably fit in one of mine."

CHAPTER 23

CARY

Thatch bounded down the stairs. Well, it sounded like it from the kitchen, and I wondered if he'd taken the steps three at a time. When he was in front of me again, slightly out of breath, I might add, he handed me a pair of green board shorts. Our fingers touched, and my mind went blank for a moment. He was wearing a tight long-sleeved white t-shirt and a pair of blue swim trunks. The fabric clung to his lean muscled frame and my mouth went dry. We stood there, enduring another staring contest, until my brain worked again.

"Damn, I was hoping for speedos." I held them out in front of me and winked. Thatch's eyes dropped, then shifted back to my face. I knew that look, but wasn't accustomed to the hint of terror lurking in his eyes. Thatch's pupils dilated, then expanded, and dilated one more time. "Just kidding. I've never owned a pair before. It must be our generation, because growing up, I would've been appalled to wear one of those skimpy things."

"You probably went to one of those snotty private schools in Manhattan where everything had to be extra proper." Thatch grinned, and I wondered how he knew that, then remembered he had an apartment in Soho.

"Of course, I did. Collegiate School, an all-boys academy until the ninth grade. After that, they sent me to the Phillips Exeter Academy in New Hampshire, where I graduated at the top of my class." I pointed my nose in the air, rolled my eyes, and laughed. "When it comes to snobs, I can outclass them every fucking time."

"Why am I not surprised?" Thatch breathed, then strolled toward the glass doors leading to the patio. I followed, and when we got outside, he pointed at a small white building. "You can change in there. Bring a couple of towels with you on the way out. They're stacked next to the door."

I walked into the changing room and sat on a bench built into the wall.

"Am I doing the right thing?" I whispered, then sat in silence for a few moments, almost like I was expecting the roof to open up and a celestial being to give me the answer, but as always, no such beings offered me their advice.

I found Thatch very attractive, and that was what frightened me. When I hooked up with younger guys, it was always easy. There was rarely an emotional connection between us beyond the desire for human contact and some spicy fun, but this was different. Thatch provoked my interest, and it wasn't just about sex.

If sex was all I wanted, I wouldn't be sitting here now wondering if I was making the right choice. I'd skip the swimsuit and strut out to the pool in all my naked glory. Get right to the point, so to speak, but if I did, it would turn Thatch off, I was sure of it. Not only that, I suspected I would be disappointed in myself for lacking self-control.

There was a crack in the white wooden wall directly ahead

of me, with a sliver of sunlight shining through. I got to my feet and peeked through it.

Thatch was pacing next to the pool. His shirt was off, and he was rubbing the back of his neck. He stopped suddenly and directed his gaze toward the changing room. I jumped back, afraid he'd catch me spying on him. If I wasn't mistaken, Thatch was just as nervous as I was, and he probably had better reasons to doubt his actions than I did.

"Tell him what Sam said when he left earlier." I muttered, then hastily stripped down and slid the swimming trunks on. Leaving my clothes on the bench, I strolled out, my heart pounding in my chest.

"Don't forget the towels!" Thatch called out, and I stumbled as I turned back to get them. I grabbed two of them from the top of the stack and forced a serene smile on my face. Whatever happened next was unfamiliar territory for me, and I wasn't about to run away from it now.

"It's a little chilly." I said, dropping the towels on one of the metal tables surrounding the pool. "Does it ever warm up?"

"Only for a couple of weeks in August. My property is in a small valley, and it keeps the temperatures cooler. Interestingly enough, occasionally there will be a snow storm, and the geography prevents much of it from falling. It covers the region in snow, and here I only get a dusting." Thatch said, then gestured toward the water. "Ready to hop in? The water is warm."

"Yeah." I mumbled, and before I could make it to the concrete steps leading into the water, Thatch cannonballed into the pool, splashing me. A second later, his head emerged from the water, and a brilliant white smile spread across his face.

"You're already wet, so hurry, get in, Cary." He said, then he laughed, but it was oddly high-pitched. He was just as nervous as I was.

If I hadn't been so nervous I would have thrown myself into

the water like he did, but instead I ambled down the steps, holding the metal railing in the middle of them for support. The deeper I got, the more the water supported me, and I felt more agile than I had been since the embolism.

"I like this," I breathed, and while I'd never been a remarkable swimmer, I found myself floating on my back, kicking with my feet to get to the other side of the pool where he was gripping the wall. Once I was next to Thatch, I faced him and without thinking blurted out what Sam talked to me about earlier.

"Your son broke up with me again."

Thatch tilted his head, and the sunlight struck his wet, silver hair. For the first time in my life I was finding a man with gray hair hot... no, more than hot. He was like a Greek god come to life.

"What the hell are you talking about, Cary?" He breathed, then combed his wet hair behind his ears.

"When you and Celia Mae went upstairs, Sam came rushing down, almost like he'd been waiting for the two of you to disappear." I closed my eyes for a moment, trying to recall exactly what he said. "He said he'd met another guy, which I thought he'd already told us the night before, but I could be wrong, but more importantly, he explained that while he thought I was a wonderful man, which is a given..."

"Good God, Cary, just stick to what my son said to you." Thatch giggled, and I had to shake my head to remember Sam's words since the color of Thatch's eyes matched the blue of the water.

"Shit, I shouldn't have brought this up."

"Don't tease me, then clam up about it. What did Sam say to you?"

"Sam said..." I took a deep breath. ".. he didn't want to get in the way of you and me." My gaze went skyward, afraid to see Thatch's reaction.

"So there's a you and me now, huh?" His voice had a lilt to it. Then I felt his hands on my shoulders, so I looked straight at him. His fingers slipped, and he held on tighter. "Do you want there to be a you and me?"

"I..."

Thatch pulled me into his chest and cut off my words with a kiss. The stubble around his mouth scraped my skin in the most delicious way, and I heard a groan coming from either me or him. Possibly both of us. His thigh slipped in between my legs and pushed up on my now firm cock, and his grip on me tightened. Only in the south had I heard the word swoon used with any regularity, and had always wondered what it meant to experience it. Now I knew, because the world faded into nothingness as I tasted Thatch for the first time. Finally, Thatch broke the kiss, and I gasped.

"Sorry, Cary. I couldn't help myself." Thatch's breath hitched, and he shook his head and tightened his hold on me. I was practically sitting on his lap underneath the water.

"For what?" I was still in a daze, and couldn't figure out what he was asking forgiveness for.

"I kissed you."

"And I kissed you back." I licked my lips, wanting more. "You can kiss me again if you w..."

My eyes snapped shut the moment his lips touched mine. This kiss was sweeter, yet more urgent. The one thing I disliked about young guys was how abrupt and awkward kissing them was, but Thatch was the opposite. Instead of tonsil diving, he nibbled my lips, then dipped his tongue into my mouth. Thatch stood up while still holding me against him, and I felt his excitement pressing against me. We were both trembling, holding on to each other as if we would drown, then a sound like a gunshot jolted us back to reality. My eyes snapped open inches from his wide-open eyes.

"Honey, I've never been with a man who could make the earth move." Thatch drawled, and this time, there was a clap of thunder. We glanced up at the same time and saw dark clouds surging overhead. "We'd best get inside. Looks like a storm is coming."

Both of our chests were heaving, as if we'd run a marathon, and I knew if we went inside I wouldn't be able to control myself. But I didn't want to, not with Thatch.

"I want you."

Thatch gazed at me with what appeared to be wonder, but knowing my luck he thought I was a fool for not getting out of the pool fast enough.

"I want you too, Cary. No lie. I haven't kissed a man, well, a passionate kiss, in years." Thatch grasped my shoulders and began pulling me to the other side of the pool. When we got to the steps, another crack of thunder hastened our exit.

Thatch got out first and tossed me a towel at the same time as heavy raindrops began to fall.

"My clothes, they're still in the…"

"You're not gonna need them, Cary. Promise."

CHAPTER 24

CARY

T hatch pulled me through the backdoor and there was a crack of thunder, so loud I clutched my chest and yelped.

"Are you okay, Cary?" Thatch grabbed my arm, then the power went out. "Oh, shit."

"It was beautiful, just a…" I began, but forgot what I was saying because I could hear what sounded like pebbles being thrown at Thatch's house. "What the hell is that?"

"Hail." Thatch's intense blue eyes bored into mine. "It never hails here, and I don't know what's going to happen to all my windows. Jesus, and the skylights. What happens if they're shattered?"

This was a serious emergency, but I was fairly sure his mansion was built to withstand it. What I couldn't, no, wouldn't accept was not seeing this thing with Thatch through to the end. No fucking way was I letting Mother Nature fuck this up. I placed my hands on his waist and pulled him into my chest.

"We're going to be fine." I spoke over the chaotic noise of

the hail, then brushed my lips over his. "Do you have some candles, because it's getting dark in here."

Thatch glanced at the window, where black clouds filled the sky. "Look at that," he pointed to the bottom of the glass door leading out to the pool. There were already a couple of inches of ice balls climbing up the door.

"Do you get tornadoes?" I asked, feeling the muscles in my legs tightening as if I were about to race away to safety, but with the astounding amount of glass the home was made of, there was probably not a safe spot to be found.

"It's very rare, but it happens." Thatch let go of me and walked into the kitchen. A moment later, he returned with a cardboard box. "C'mon, let's go upstairs. These are my Christmas candles. We're going to need them. Plus..." he leaned down and kissed me under my ear, "...storm or no storm, you are coming to my bed."

My knees felt weak, and I wasn't sure if it was the storm, or his words.

When we reached his room, Thatch opened the box and began placing candles throughout it. It was dark, so I couldn't see much of his space, but I noticed that the intensity of the hail had lessened.

"Help me with the candles," Thatch said, and handed me a lighter. Less than a minute later, the room was filled with flickering shadows and a golden glow.

"How are you feeling?" Thatch walked up to me for what I thought was going to be a kiss, but instead he picked up my wrist and held it for a minute.

"What are you doing? Taking my pulse?"

"Well, you had a health emergency just a..."

"And it wasn't my heart." I chuckled at his concern.

"It's racing." Thatch pulled me into his chest, and I felt his heart pounding against mine. "You know, I haven't had another man sleep in my bed since my div... shit. Why am I talking about my divorce? It's the world's biggest turnoff."

"Actually, I haven't spent a full night in bed with another man in decades. I prefer to sleep alone."

"Really?"

"Yeah," I whispered, then brushed my lips over Thatch's cheek. "Why am I suddenly terrified? It's not like I've never done this before."

"Make love? It's always scary the first time you're with someone." Thatch's hand dropped to my ass and squeezed. "Did you take one of your boner pills? Because I can feel that you want to be with me."

"No. This is all your doing, Thatch." I pushed my erection against the top of his leg and felt his cock poking at my stomach. "Let's stop talking about my medical issues before Mr. Happy goes bye-bye."

"It's a deal." He breathed, then his lips hovered over mine for a moment, and it was almost like he was asking for my permission to kiss me.

"Please, I want you." I whispered, and Thatch's lips pressed against mine. It was light at first, a kiss you'd give your mother, or a friend, then his mouth opened and our tongues met, swirling against each other, and I realized no one had ever kissed me like this before. It wasn't the frantic, awkward kiss I was used to getting from inexperienced or drunk twinks.

"Your lips are so soft," I breathed, pulling back a moment to catch my breath.

"I'm glad they still work." Thatch said, then shivered. We were still in our damp swimsuits. "My lips are used to eating, whistling, making..."

I shushed him with my mouth, nibbling on the side of his neck as he clung to me. Thatch's legs shook, and he groaned, a sexy deep sound that sent a shiver up my spine. I moved my lips up and down the arch of his neck, from his ear down to his chest and back again, sucking his skin hard.

"I can't take it anymore. That's too good." He pushed me back, panting. "Jesus, we aren't even naked yet and I feel like I'm about to completely lose it."

A crack of thunder ripped through the air, and instead of hailstones, sheets of rain pummeled the house. I fingered the front of the swimsuit, wanting to yank them off, but feeling shy. Thatch's eyes followed my hand, and he must have noticed my hesitation. He dropped to his knees in front of me and mouthed my cock through the damp material.

"Thatch, oh my God, I want to feel your mouth on my cock so damned bad," I hissed. Then, he undid the velcro in the front and pulled them down to my knees.

"Yes," Thatch sighed, gripping the base of my shaft. "I've been going crazy, alone in this bedroom, wanting to taste you." He licked the tip of my cock, then slid it into his mouth. My fingers laced through his hair as he engulfed more of my length. I glanced down and our eyes met.

"Damn, it's like you really, really want it, don't you?" I purred, and another inch disappeared into his throat. This was so different from what I was used to. Thatch knew what he was doing, instead of the accidental bites and awkward fumbles of younger men. I kept watching him while he worked my cock, and by now he'd freed his dick and was working it with his fist. It was as big as I hoped it would be. Not too big you couldn't do anything with it, and thick enough so I'd feel its heft once I got it in my hands. Watching him suck my cock while jerking his dick was bringing me close to the edge. It had been too long since I'd had a man who knew what he was doing in bed.

"Slow down." I slid my hands to the sides of his head and gently pushed him off of me. A stream of spit was leaking from the corner of his mouth, and I pulled him to his feet with his armpits and covered his lips with mine. He tasted sweet, like he'd been eating hard candies before we'd ended up in his bedroom. The kiss grew intense, hot, bordering on sloppy. And suddenly I fell forward, my ankles tangled up in the swimsuit I'd forgotten to kick off.

"Shit," I muttered, and Thatch cracked up laughing, catching me before I fell to the floor. It took me a moment, but I freed myself from the damp fabric, kicking it across the room. "Why does this feel so awkward, yet so damned right?"

"It definitely feels right." Thatch murmured, then he took off his swim trunks, sat on the bed and pulled me on top of him. "You feel awkward, because you're used to being in control."

"Huh?"

"C'mon, you got to admit that being with young guys guaranteed that you would run the show. Now you're making love with an equal, both in age and, well, maybe not experience." Thatch's blue eyes twinkled, and a sheepish smile spread across his cheeks. "I've only been with a handful of men before."

"You certainly know what you're doing." I pecked him on the nose, then fell off of him, stretching my body next to his. I draped my arm across his chest and hugged him tight.

"Well, I might not have been with a lot of guys, but that doesn't mean I wasn't making love often. Though I must admit to feeling insecure right now. You've probably got a lot more experience than I do." Thatch mumbled, and I detected a hint of shame in his timbre.

"You have more experience where it counts," I murmured, and kissed his nipple. "You keep referring to sex as making love. What does that even mean?"

"You've never been in love before?" Thatch turned on his side, facing me. He kissed my forehead, then my nose, and flitted his lips across mine while I decided how to best answer the question.

"No," I sighed. "I've had many crushes, but I've never understood what love is. Educate me. First, tell me what you mean by the term making love. How is that different from having sex?"

Thatch inhaled, then breathed out a warm stream of air on my cheek. "Why do you make me think and feel so much?" He sighed. "Well, sex is different for everyone, so I'm defining the term making love based on my experiences."

"Can I tell you something?" I reached over and stroked his arm. "Don't listen to Sam when he tells you to stop talking like a geek. You're an intelligent man, and it's rare for me to encounter one, especially a man as smart and handsome as you."

Thatch's glossy blue eyes met mine, and he reached over and stroked my cheek. "Thank you. You're pretty smart too. Making love is almost like an art, practiced between two people who have deep feelings for one another. It doesn't require that the two, or more I guess, people be in a committed relationship. Making love is about exploring an emotional connection between them while having sex."

"So I guess getting off isn't an important part of it, right?"

"It's not a requirement, but when I make love to a man, they almost always do." Thatch said, then reached over and grasped my shaft in his hand. "For me it's about being in the moment, expressing how I feel using my body, and my partner's."

"Will you show me? You know, how this making love stuff works?" I shut my eyes for a moment, then felt Thatch shift in the bed. When I opened my eyes, he was climbing on top of me, then his knees spread my legs apart.

"There's nothing I want more right now than to make love to you, Cary Lancaster."

CHAPTER 25

THATCH

As I bent down to kiss Cary, his eyes fluttered shut. This man was proving to be the opposite of what I'd originally believed about him. Yes, I'd always thought he was sexy, but I'd also thought he was a cad, a preening peacock who only cared about himself.

My mouth crashed into his, and Cary's legs wrapped around my waist, pulling me down closer to him. He groaned into my mouth, and my cock now felt like a steel rod. I propped myself up with a hand on each side of Cary's shoulders, and our tongues swirled together, exploring each other's mouths.

I didn't understand how anyone could get to Cary's age and claim that they'd never been in love before, or had never made love to anyone. It was like a challenge for me, and I wanted to show this handsome multi-faceted man how much better sex was when there were intense feelings behind the physical act itself.

I broke off the kiss, and Cary's dark eyes opened, fixed directly on mine.

"So, you are making love to me now?" Cary whispered,

then there was a crack of thunder. We both froze, and seconds later the bright, blue-and-white light of lightning illuminated the room for a brief flash.

"Yes." I nuzzled Cary's neck, pressing down on his erection with my own. "You are so beautiful." I murmured and meant it. He didn't seem like the type to spend hours at a gym, but his skin was tan, and he had a natural musculature most men his age would love to have.

"You are too, Thatch," Cary replied, then gasped as I continued pressing down on his cock. I wanted to taste him again, so I moved further down his frame until his girth was underneath my mouth. I licked the tip, and another bolt of lightning illuminated the room. His hips arched, and I took the first inch of his shaft in my mouth. I felt his fingers in my hair, then I engulfed the rest of his length.

"Oh my God," Cary hissed, and I tasted his excitement. I began working his shaft, using only my lips and mouth, and soon his hips were bucking, forcing his cock inside me even deeper. "You're going to make me come, Thatch."

I stopped, letting his shaft slip out of my mouth, hitting his stomach with a whack. "Isn't that the point?"

"No, not yet." Cary panted. "It's my turn to taste you."

With energy I didn't think he possessed, Cary sat up and pushed me down beside him on my back, then straddled my waist. When I met his gaze, there was a look of wonder on his face. Cary's eyes were wide, his cheeks flushed, and beads of sweat dotted his forehead.

"I don't know what you've done to me, Thatch, but I've wanted no one as much as I do you, right now." Cary sighed. "Is that part of making love? This need? Because, I only want to please you."

A loud boom rocked the house, and almost immediately afterward, blue light flashed from outside. Then I heard something crash against one of my windows, and we both jumped. A small tree branch was being held against the window beside us by the wind, which was howling.

"Part of me is terrified," Cary murmured. "But, it's not the storm."

I reached above me, grabbed his shoulders, and pulled him down into an embrace. Cary's heart was racing, and so was mine. "This was meant to be handsome. Our first time together, and Mother Nature is either pissed off at us, or she is celebrating it."

Cary's breath was hot against my cheek, and I felt his entire body shudder. He licked the side of my neck, then began kissing his way down the side of my body until his face was over my cock. He blew on it, sending a shiver up my spine, then he grasped my shaft and covered the tip with his mouth. Cary groaned, and the vibrations felt electric. He took another inch into his mouth and began working my cock with both his hands and mouth.

"This is heaven," I sighed, and felt Cary's other hand cupping my balls and gently squeezing them. His tongue swirled around the head of my dick, and I wondered how much longer I could last. It had been years since I'd been with a man, and I could already feel the sparks of my orgasm approaching.

"Cary, I'm getting close." I muttered, and instead of slowing down, he increased the pace. I gripped the sheets, struggling to stay in control, but the pressure building under my groin told me I was about to shoot my load. "Please, Cary, I'm going to…"

Abruptly, he stopped, still holding my shaft in his fist. Cary glanced up, his face wet. Our eyes met, and I saw something beneath his lustful gaze. His brown eyes were glowing in the golden light of the candles, wet and warm. He took my cock in his mouth again, and I felt my toes curl.

"Please, Jesus, Cary I'm..." I began, but my head started thrashing to the left and right, and I couldn't form the words. My come was snaking its way up my shaft, and at any moment I knew I would lose it. Without thinking, my fingers laced through his thick salt-and-pepper hair, and I held him still, praying I could keep my orgasm at bay. I didn't want this to end so soon.

Cary released my cock and grinned up at me. Then, to my surprise, he stretched out beside me, kissed my nipple, and said, "I want you inside me."

I would've sworn he was a top, and couldn't imagine him allowing someone else to have control over his body. "Are you sure?"

"It's been almost twenty years since I bottomed for another man, but something tells me you'd..."

Before he could finish his sentence, I was on top of him, my mouth covering his while I ground my cock into his groin. Another crack of thunder sounded, and Cary wrapped his arms around my sides and pulled me into him. When I broke the kiss, we both struggled to catch our breath. Without another word, I reached over to my nightstand and pulled out a box of condoms, and prayed they were still good. I'd bought them a couple of years ago when I was determined to do something about my lackluster sex life. Eyeing them, I frantically searched for an expiration date, and thankfully they still had a couple of months before going out of date. I pulled one out of the box and yanked a bottle of lube out of the drawer. With shaking hands, I sheathed myself, then noticed Cary had his hands behind his head and was staring at me with a bemused smile on his face.

"What?"

"Nothing, I'm just enjoying the view." He reached up and stroked my chest as I positioned myself in between his legs. I placed his legs over my shoulders and gazed down into his glistening eyes.

"If you'd told me we'd end up here, together, when we first met, I would've laughed you out of my house." I murmured, placing the head of my cock against his entrance. "But, now I can't imagine anyone else I'd rather have here in my arms."

"Don't be gentle," Cary whispered. "I want to feel your passion, Thatch. Make me yours."

I bit my lower lip and pushed inside him, stopping when he grimaced. "Are you okay?"

"Yes, just give me a second." Cary shut his eyes and breathed in and out a few times, then I felt him relax, and when his eyes opened again, I pushed inside more.

"Wow," Cary breathed, and a smile spread across his cheeks. "More, Thatch. Give me all of you."

My entire body trembled at the thought of being all the way inside him, to be as one with this man in a way I hadn't been with anyone else in years. Cary's hands gripped the sheets, and as I pushed deeper into him, a bolt of lightning flashed outside. When the burst of thunder followed, neither of us jumped. We trained our eyes on each other, and finally I was inside him to the hilt. I shivered, leaned down, and kissed the tip of his nose. A bead of sweat dropped from my forehead, landing next to his full lips.

"Please, Thatch. Make love to me."

My eyes closed, and I felt his muscles tightening their grip around my cock, then I pulled almost all the way out, and slammed back in to the hilt.

"Yes, oh my God, yes," Cary said, and when I opened my eyes, his teeth were gritted. "Show me how you feel, Thatch. Take me now, I'm yours."

Something in his words triggered me, and a loud groan ripped through me as I began ramming my cock in and out of his tight warmth. Cary held on to my shoulders as I rode him, and soon my mouth was over his, but I couldn't quite reach his lips. Rain pelted the windows, and the wind howled. The only other sounds were our groans and the sound of our sweaty bodies slapping against one another.

"Jesus!" Cary cried, and he froze underneath me. His muscles gripped my cock, and when I looked down, come was shooting up his chest. Seeing his face twisted in pleasure sent me over the edge, and my thighs pulled back and I pounded him in earnest.

"Yes, yes, oh damn it, fuck me, Thatch." Cary's strangled voice yelled out, and I felt my come rocketing up my cock and into him.

"Heaven help me," I cried. My cock kept pistoning into him while the built-up pressure dissipated, and finally I collapsed on top of him, panting for air.

Cary held me tight, then his fingers went to my hair, stroking me while I recovered from possibly the most electric orgasm of my life.

"You are beautiful, Thatch," Cary whispered. I raised my head enough to see his eyes.

"No, no, I'm not." My eyes shut again, a strange shyness coming over me.

"You are to me. C'mon, open your eyes, so I know you can hear me." Cary's baritone crooned. I obliged and was shocked to see a tear snaking down the side of his nose. Leaning down, I kissed it away.

"I don't know what's wrong with me. Why am I crying?"

"Nothing's wrong with you, Cary. Absolutely nothing." I got off of him, swung one leg over his thighs and laid my head on his chest. The hair on his chest was coming in, a mixture of black and white hairs now long enough they felt soft against my cheek. His body shook, and I realized he was silently sobbing. Holding him tighter, I let him cry, because I had a feeling they weren't tears of sadness.

———

The sound of my cell phone buzzing jolted me out of a deep slumber. My eyes popped open, and a wave of disappointment rolled through me.

Cary was gone. He'd told me he never went to sleep with anyone, so he was probably in his room. There was only one candle still burning making it hard to see. I found my phone on the nightstand and saw that it was Sam. Not in the mood for texting, I placed a call to him instead.

"Dad, are you guys alright?"

"Yeah. Why?" I yawned, my head sinking back into the pillow.

"It was all over the news. A bunch of freak tornados in your area, and one of them hit the Biltmore Estate." I glanced up at the skylight over the bed and saw branches and debris covering it, plus the electricity hadn't come back on. The white light of the moon shone through the branches, meaning the storm had passed. I'd have to call the landscape crew tomorrow to come clean up the mess.

"Oh that. No, Sam, we're fine. Promise." I mumbled, struggling to keep my eyes open.

"Are you having sex with Cary?"

"What?" I croaked, realizing I couldn't fool my son. "Um, no, we aren't having sex right now."

"Oh my God," Sam giggled. "But, you did, didn't you?"

My silence spoke for me.

"Was it amazing? Because it's been so long since you…"

"Goodnight Sam. Love you." My son screamed something unintelligible, and I hung up before he could say anything else.

Then the bedroom door opened a few inches and Cary stuck his head through it.

"Come in," I sang out, grinning like a fool.

Cary's eyes were wide, and I imagined what he looked like as a young boy.

"Hey, I stood in front of Sam's door for what seemed like forever and realized I was, well, shortchanging myself. So instead of staying there I came back. I know I said I didn't like to sleep with anyone, but would you mind if I tried with you?"

CHAPTER 26

CARY

A sudden hum jolted me awake. I opened my eyes and realized I was in bed with Thatch, his arms wrapped around me from behind. What did they call this again? Spooning?

"Good morning," Thatch murmured, pulling me closer against his body. "The electricity just came back on." He yawned. "Could you hand me my phone? It's next to you on the nightstand."

I did as he asked, and when I saw the time on the screen, I was pleasantly surprised. "Wow. This is probably the longest I've slept in years." According to his phone, we'd slept for ten hours. "Maybe I should always sleep with someone. Haven't felt this rested in my life."

"I never sleep more than four or five hours, so yes, this is a miracle." Thatch kissed the back of my neck and sighed. "Or it could be the company."

"The doctor is visiting today. Joey thinks I should be good enough to leave." I said and realized I didn't want to go back to

Raleigh. Hell, I'd barely lived there before coming here, and this felt much more like home to me now.

"That's because Joey wants you out of the picture so he can ravish me." Thatch giggled, and I felt something hard slip in between my legs. Instantly I felt my cock firm up. Not only that, but I was feeling sore, like I'd been riding a horse for days on end. "Little does he know that I've been ravishing you instead."

"Ah, so you have other suitors." I laughed. "Oh my God, I'm starting to sound like you, all southern fancy schmancy."

"What time are they getting here?"

"Three. We have a few more hours. Why not spend them in bed?" I languidly replied, loving the feel of Thatch's arms around me. Whenever I tried to have sleepovers with twinks, I always ended up leaving in the middle of the night. Could never fall asleep with them, but Thatch was like a walking sex machine and sleeping pill all rolled into one.

"I wish we could, but I have things to do." Thatch let go of me, and I felt him sitting up in bed. I groaned in protest, then sat up too. "Shit, look at that." He pointed out the window. There was a tree down, and what had been bucolic scenery was now a chaotic disaster.

"At least your house held up." I said, taking his hand in mine.

"We don't know that, which is why I must inspect it and the property. I'm wondering if the driveway is even passable. If it isn't, you might have to reschedule your doctor's visit." Thatch's voice lifted on that last sentence, and I prayed every single tree lining his driveway was now blocking it. We stayed like this silently for a good two minutes, neither of us wanting to break the romantic spell we'd cast together. Finally, Thatch patted my thigh and climbed out of the bed with a groan.

"Take your time getting up," he said, then walked over to

his dresser and pulled out a pair of gray sweatpants and a matching hoodie. "I'll go to the kitchen and put on some coffee. Maybe I'll make us some pancakes, too."

As he put on the clothes, I stared at him, wondering what the hell was happening to me. I'd spent decades alone, or with guys I never felt much for. Now the thought of him just going downstairs was depressing me.

"What?" Thatch grinned. "You're looking at me like you have a question."

"Oh, no. Sorry." I scooted down and pulled the blankets over my head. "I'll be downstairs in a few minutes. Gotta go take some pills in Sam's room."

I heard his feet padding across the room and felt his weight on the mattress as he sat down next to me. Thatch pulled the blankets back, and I grinned up at him. Without thinking, I said, "I feel like a better person when you're around."

"Oh really?" Thatch's smile split his face. I reached up and stroked his morning stubble. "That makes two of us." He pecked me on the cheek, then pulled the covers back over my head. "See you downstairs."

———

For a few more minutes, I contemplated getting out of bed. I needed to pee, and a cup of coffee would help me get motivated to see my damned doctor and the jealous nurse. I pulled the covers back and swung my feet to the floor.

"Ouch," I groaned. When I got to the door, I leaned against the wall for a minute, unused to that just-fucked feeling that made my legs so wobbly. "You definitely are a big boy, Thatch." I grinned, then held on to the wall as I made my way to Sam's bedroom. When I opened his door, I gasped.

Three windows were busted, and glass, leaves, and

branches were scattered across the room. "How the hell did we not hear it?"

I found my phone, then maneuvered around the debris to the bathroom and grabbed my pills off the counter. Before heading downstairs, I threw on some clothes and snapped a picture to show Thatch the damage.

When I got to the kitchen, Thatch was whistling, and true to his word there was coffee already made. He was stirring batter in a large blue ceramic bowl.

"I hate to tell you this, but some of Sam's windows are broken, and there's crap all over the place." I showed him the picture I'd taken, then poured myself a cup of coffee.

"Shit," Thatch muttered, and to my surprise, he grinned. "Well, hopefully that's the worst of it."

"You also have made me into a semi-invalid again." I winced as I sat down by the counter. "My ass is sore."

Thatch came over and patted my shoulder. "It's like riding a bicycle, you…"

"No, it was like riding a horse. Trust me." I winked, and Thatch's cheeks turned pink. "In a good way, honey."

He bit his lower lip, then kissed me. Hard, like he wanted to throw me over his shoulder, take me to his cave, and fuck me all over again. My heart pounded, and my hands flew to his chest, pulling him closer to me. When he broke the kiss, my eyes were still closed, and my lips were pursed together. I probably looked like one of those kissing fish people kept in aquariums.

"What was that for?" I breathed, and a little tremor shot through my body.

"You called me honey." Thatch winked. "Well, and your comment has brought out the rooster in me." He waggled his eyebrows, and if my eyes weren't mistaken, there was a bit of a swagger to him I hadn't noticed before.

When he strolled over to the refrigerator, I could see a difference in how he was carrying himself, and the eggplant in his sweats was noticeably bigger.

"Look outside at the pool." Thatch instructed, and I gingerly stood up, so I could get a better view.

"Oh, shit." There were so many leaves in it you couldn't see the water. Oh, and there were two large multi-colored umbrellas floating on top of the leaves from the patio furniture. "How the hell did all this happen, and we heard none of it?"

"We were busy." Thatch walked over and patted my ass. "And to my surprise, I'm not even upset about the damage. It's the price you pay for good lovin'. Plus, I have excellent insurance and a crew of landscapers who'll clean the mess for me."

"Have you looked through the rest of the house?" I asked.

"Not yet. I'm not letting this get to me. We're safe, that's what matters the most. C'mon, let me finish breakfast and then we can walk around the property and see the damage first hand. Oh, and I need to call the cleaning service. Normally they come every week, but since you've been here, I've been doing most of it myself." Thatch said, then went back to stirring the batter. That was when my phone buzzed. Instead of looking at it, I sat and sipped my coffee.

"Aren't you going to get that?" Thatch asked, turning on the stove.

"Yeah, sure," I mumbled, not wanting to. I picked it up and saw messages from Jenny, and a fresh one from Dr. Creighton. Since she was coming over later, I tapped her message first.

Sorry I have to cancel your appointment for this afternoon Emergency room is packed because of the storm last night

"Anything important?" Thatch asked, pouring pancake batter onto a cast-iron skillet.

I didn't know how to react to Dr. Creighton's message. Part of me wanted to stay here with Thatch longer, but I didn't want to become an unwelcome guest, either. What was that saying again?

"Guests, like fish, begin to smell after three days." I murmured.

"What was that? Couldn't hear you." Thatch grinned. Damn it, I wanted to stay, but I didn't want to be a smelly old fish either. I inhaled, then told him what the doctor said.

"Dr. Creighton canceled my appointment because of the storm."

CHAPTER 27

THATCH

"Oh, that's too bad." I tried to keep the relief out of my voice, but Cary's raised eyebrow showed me I'd failed. "It's not a big deal, Cary. I guess it means you'll be staying a little longer."

"The pancake is burning." Cary pointed at the skillet.

"Shit," I muttered, then grabbed a spatula and removed the nearly black pancake. After tossing it out, I poured more batter on the skillet and lowered the heat. "Actually, that might be for the best, since we don't know if the driveway is even passable yet." I said, struggling to keep my voice neutral. Yes, the storm had caused a lot of damage, but there was a silver lining. Our time together was extended, and maybe, just maybe, Cary would want more than a tumble in the sheets.

"You know, I can always have Jenny arrange for the clean-up of your property." Cary said, then sipped his coffee.

"Why? I have my own people who can handle this." I noticed the little bubbles on the pancake had popped, so I flipped it over.

"Well, if you're using locals, don't they have other clients to take care of? I'm sure they're going to be super busy over the next few weeks. Jenny's job is to take care of stuff like this, and trust me, she can have a team of abuelas cleaning this place up within hours." Cary grinned, and I shook my head in confusion.

"What do you mean? A team of grandmothers will fly in and clean the place?"

"If you want the job done right, hire older Mexican women. They will even vacuum your driveway if you ask them to. I always pay them double the going rate and I'm never disappointed by their work. Plus, I owe you for allowing me, a perfect stranger, to recover here. Let me take care of it, I insist." Cary held his hands out and smiled. While I appreciated his offer, I was unsure of taking him up on it. Selfishly, I wanted him to stay as long as possible.

"Well, um…"

"Pancake, Thatch." Cary pointed at the pancake, which was on the verge of burning. I placed it on a plate and slid it in front of him.

"Let me get the syrup," I mumbled. It was in the pantry, and while I was in there, I stood still with my eyes shut for a moment, collecting my thoughts. After last night, I didn't want whatever was happening between us to end. I wanted to stop time, or go backwards to a point before the storm. Soon my house would be overrun by landscape crews, and if Cary had his way, a gaggle of Mexican grandmothers. I grabbed the bottle of maple syrup and went back to the kitchen.

"Let's walk around the property first before making any decisions. Also, I have to consult with Brian about it." I placed the bottle in front of him, then poured more batter into the skillet.

"Why do you have to speak to him?" Cary asked. "It's not

like he's living here or helping you out." His lips pressed into a straight line, and I detected an edge to his voice.

"Because it's our house, not just mine. Yes, he spends most of his time in New York or at Nags Head, but when it comes to large repairs, he has to be consulted."

"Oh." Cary mumbled, then grabbed his fork and knife and began slicing up his pancake. "You should buy his share of the house. He's not a very…. Never mind."

"One of the reasons we shared the property after the divorce was Sam." I sighed, then flipped the pancake. "When Brian and I split up, we wanted to present a united front for our son. Though I must admit, enough time has passed… let's finish eating, then look around. Hopefully, there isn't much damage besides Sam's room."

———

Cary came out of Sam's room dressed like an exotic french sailor, and before I could stop myself, I laughed.

"What's so funny?" Cary asked, a slow smile spreading across his face. "I'm wearing what Jenny sent me. I don't have country clothes."

"Come back to my room for a sec." I said, and moments later I was pulling a sturdy pair of bright yellow wellies out of the closet. Cary made a face when I handed them to him.

"No offense, but I haven't worn this type of boot since I was a child." Cary sat on the edge of the bed and slid his loafers off.

"Remember, there was a storm, which means mud. You don't want to mess up your nice shoes." I suppressed a grin, not telling him that snakes and other critters tended to be more active after such a big storm.

"Fine." He grumbled, pulling on the bright yellow boots. "They're a little too big, but I'll manage."

A few minutes later, we were walking out of the garage.

"Holy shit." I muttered, then forced myself back to the serene head space I'd had earlier. Fallen branches and leaves covered the driveway for as far as I could see. An ancient oak tree I'd always loved was lying across the middle of it a hundred yards in front of us. Placing an arm over Cary's shoulder, I stated the obvious. "Well, your doctor wouldn't be able to make it up the driveway, so that cancellation was the smart thing for her to do."

I felt his arm go around my waist. "Yeah, but damn, I feel sorry for all the work that has to be done. Your pool is a mess, the driveway, Sam's room. We need to call some landscapers, so why don't we go back inside and inspect the rest of the house? Plus, I'd swear I just felt a raindrop."

We both glanced up and a sprinkle of rain fell on our faces. I sighed, then grabbed Cary's hand. "C'mon. You've been here for days now and you still haven't seen much of the house."

"Okay," Cary mumbled. "Look, I meant what I said earlier. Jenny is an expert on this type of stuff. Let me take care of it for you. It's the least I can do."

I glanced down at him and smiled. He was either determined to get out of here as fast as he could, or he really meant to take care of this mess for me. "If I say yes, I want to pay for it."

Cary rolled his eyes, then said, "Yes, sir. I'll have Jenny pay for it, and you can reimburse me if you must. But, I just want you to know I'd prefer to do it as a way of saying thank you." He stopped walking, then opened his arms and hugged me tight. "Thanks for everything, and I'm not just referring to the excellent food. For last night, and for…"

"Hush," I whispered, then pecked him on the cheek. "I'm scared to see my office. There are so many windows. I can only imagine how bad the damage might be."

"Everything can be fixed, just remember that. C'mon, let's get it over with. Then we can go back to bed." Cary winked, and bit his lower lip.

"You like me, huh? Like, you really like me?" I blurted, and Cary pulled me back into his embrace.

"Can you feel how much I like you?" He whispered, and I felt his cock pressed against my thigh. "Trust me, I do."

As we toured the house, I showed him the playroom, complete with a bar, pool tables, and pinball machines. It was in the basement, so I assumed it would have survived the storm unscathed, but I was wrong. The floors were slick with muddy water, and the carpets would have to be replaced, but to my relief, the guest rooms were all intact. When we got to my office, I reached for the doorknob and stopped.

"What's wrong?" Cary asked.

I hesitated for a second. "Well, nobody is ever allowed in here. It's where I get all my creative work done. Not Sam, Brian, nor Celia Mae has ever been inside it."

"You don't have to explain. It's like your sacred space, or a geek man cave." Cary held his hands out and smiled. "I can wait here, or anywhere else you want me to."

At that moment, I realized I wanted to share it with him. Why not show him all of me, instead of keeping it off-limits like I did with everyone else? I said nothing, then turned the doorknob. "After you, Cary."

He hesitated, then walked past me into my domain. I held my breath a moment, praying nothing had been damaged, then Cary stuck his head through the door and grinned. "I see nothing amiss."

"Oh, thank God," I murmured, then followed him inside. Aside from the coffee cup on my desk that I'd forgotten to wash, everything looked fine.

"Well, look at that." Cary pointed to the framed plaque on

the wall behind my desk. "The Booker Prize. All it needs is a Pulitzer and a Nobel to go with it."

I chuckled. "While I would appreciate them, I am content with my one literary award. Surprised I got it, actually. It's almost always given to a writer from the Commonwealth of Nations, and the United States isn't one of them." I walked behind my desk and sat down. "I swear Brian fucked somebody behind my back so I'd win the award."

"While I don't know your ex very well, that wouldn't surprise me in the least."

I tilted my head, confused.

"What I mean is it has a reputation for being all about politics, the people you know, and publishers greasing palms. None of it is true, of course." Cary hastened to add the last part, then I switched on the power to my computer. Moments later, the screen was filled with messages, all from Brian. I clicked on Zoom, and to my surprise, my ex-husband's face suddenly filled the screen.

"Thank God!" Brian exclaimed. "I was worried sick about the house."

"There's been some damage, but nothing we can't fix." I sighed, then noticed Brian's eyebrows lift.

"Is that Cary Lancaster behind you?" He asked, and I felt Cary lean over my shoulder and wave his fingers at the screen.

"Hello, Brian. Long time no see." Cary grinned, and Brian scowled.

"What the hell is he doing in your fucking office? Hell, I've never been inside of it and now you have the man who sold your contract, nearly ruining your..."

"Whoah, Brian. I can have whoever I want in my house." I took a deep breath, trying to keep my emotions in check.

"Our house." Brian said through gritted teeth.

"Maybe I should wait outside." Cary said in a stage whisper, then he waved at Brian again and walked out of the office. Did Brian and Cary have a past I was unaware of? Like, beyond the publishing business? Because, Brian was acting even more like a douche than usual.

"Thatch, we need to talk, and you won't like what I have to say."

CHAPTER 28

THATCH

"Sam told me about the older man he'd been seeing, but he never disclosed his name. Is Cary that man? The one who almost died in his bed?" Brian opened the top drawer of his desk, pulled out a pint of whiskey, and poured it liberally into his coffee.

"Yes, Cary was that man. They didn't have a serious relationship, and Sam ended it right after Cary got home from the hospital." I replied. "Why are your panties in a bunch over Cary Lancaster? He's a great guy."

Brian's mouth dropped open, then he combed his fingers through his hair but he said nothing. Something told me that this was going to be quite the conversation, and Brian's whiskey made my mouth water.

"Brian, give me a minute." I rose from my seat before he could protest, and went to the door of my office and opened it. Cary was leaning against the wall in the hallway, and a languid smile spread across his face when he saw me.

"I need booze for this conversation." I sighed. "Cary, would you mind listening to Brian and I talking, but without letting him know you are there? Something is bugging me about him, and I think you have something to do with it."

"Actually, no. I don't feel comfortable doing that. This is between you and him, and whatever he says about me isn't all that important in the scheme of things." Cary stated quietly, then caressed my cheek. "You need to hear him out and make your own decisions. Personally, I think he's a pompous ass. You can do better than him."

"It's not like we're together anymore." I sighed, and Cary placed his hands around my neck and brushed his lips over mine.

Then he stared into my eyes, and murmured, "Are you sure about that?"

―――――

I grabbed a bottle of beer out of the fridge and sat behind my desk. Brian was drumming his fingers impatiently.

"Okay, tell me what's on your mind."

"Is he still in your office?" Brian asked.

"No, he isn't. It's just you and me, Brian. Now tell me, what's bugging you about Cary?" My stomach was churning, wondering what the hell was going on with my ex. I popped open the beer and took a swig of it.

Brian shook his head slowly back and forth, and his initial irritated look vanished, replaced by the smugness of a preacher lecturing his flock. "You've never been good at business, Thatch. Never had that killer instinct. That's why I've always looked out for you. For us, I mean, and Sam."

"Okay," I drew out the words, wondering where this conversation was headed.

"Remember when Cadmus started selling the contracts of

all its authors, and how I spent months trying to block the sale of yours?"

I nodded and motioned for him to continue.

"I was at a party thrown by Amanda Cornwell, who was the publicity director for Cadmus. She was as against the sale as I was, but decided to butter up Cary by inviting him, too. She thought if he could talk to the authors, editors, and agents and discover that they were more than numbers on a spreadsheet, he might reconsider shutting down Cadmus." Brian said, gesturing with both hands. This was unusual, since he normally didn't speak with his hands. I also noticed the pitch of his voice was higher.

"Obviously it didn't work." I tilted my head, curious about what he would say next. "By the way, where was I during all this? I don't recall being invited to Amanda's party."

"You were in Asheville. Sam was still in high school, so you weren't in New York often." Brian said while fidgeting with a paper clip. He was twisting it in his fingers, and then it snapped in two. He winced, and inwardly I smiled.

"Okay, that sounds about right." I muttered, remembering how difficult things had been between us at the time. He spent most of his time in New York, always making up excuses for why he couldn't be with me and Sam.

"After the party, a few of us went to a bar." Brian's gaze was somewhere over my shoulder, and for the first time in years, I doubted he was telling me the truth. "Cary was one of them."

"Okay. So you and a bunch of people from Cadmus went to a bar. What's the…?"

"Stop interrupting." He held his palm up. "Let me tell the story."

I held both my hands up in mock surrender.

"We'd all had too much to drink by then, and Cary mentioned his apartment was on the next block, so we all went back to his place. A few drinks later, and the only two people still partying were me and him. Everyone else had left. That's when Cary put the jam on me." Brian bit his lower lip, and I almost burst out laughing. There was no way in hell Cary would make a pass at Brian.

"You've got to be kidding me." I bit back a smile, then sipped my beer to hide my expression.

"He said if I would sleep with him, he'd reconsider selling your contract. Of course, I said no. I had you and Sam to think about."

Beer sprayed all over my computer screen.

"What? Why do you think this is funny?" Brian's eyebrows drew together, but when I tried to meet his gaze, he kept his eyes focused on that same place over my shoulder. My shoulders shook as I tried to stop laughing, but it was proving impossible. Brian obviously didn't know Cary well enough to know he never slept with guys his age. Well, until me.

"You're such a fucking liar, Brian." I rubbed my temples as my amusement transformed into rage. Knowing Cary the way I did, I could imagine that the opposite had happened. Brian made the moves on Cary, who turned him down cold. This was his way of spinning the story, a story Cary hadn't bothered to tell me. Why? Because, it wouldn't have crossed his mind to deliberately harm me by sharing Brian's faithlessness.

"I am not lying." Brian gestured with both hands again. "That man controlled my future, and..."

"Shut up." I shook my head back and forth, wondering if I should just end the call now or hear more of his lies. "It was both our futures at stake, and I can almost guarantee that you wanted to fuck Cary, and he told you to go to hell. If anything, you hastened his decision to sell my contract."

"That, that's not..."

I ended the video chat before he could say anything else to piss me off.

"Jesus, we were still together then, and had a teenage boy to take care of. Turns out he left me in North Carolina, so he could go to parties and fuck whoever he wanted." I picked up the beer bottle, and seconds later, what was left in it was foaming over my fingers. "Fuck!" I threw it across the room.

"Knock knock." I glanced up and saw Cary standing in the doorway of my office. "Are you okay?"

"Hand me that rag on the bar." I barked, and Cary's eyes widened. He strolled over to the bar, picked up the rag, and gave it to me. I wiped off the desk and the computer screen, all the while willing myself to calm down.

"Do you want to talk about it, or should I leave?" Cary asked, then picked up the bottle on the floor and set it on the counter.

"Sit." I gestured toward the sofa against the wall of glass. Cary sat, and I got to my feet and began pacing the room. "He accused you of trying to sleep with him, which I know is a lie."

"Yes, that's definitely not true." Cary murmured.

"So what happened?" I sat next to him and felt pressure building behind my eyes.

"It's simple. I was invited to a party some woman who worked for me threw. I left after an hour and went home. A couple of hours later, my doorman called and told me a drunk man was in the lobby. It was Brian. The doorman threatened to call the cops if he didn't leave. I told him to send him up to my place, figuring he could sleep it off in the guest room. Instead, Brian got handsy with me. When I turned him down, he stormed out. That's it. End of the story." Cary placed his hand on my knee and squeezed it. "I didn't know him well, just knew he was your agent. I didn't even know you two were married."

I sighed, because that sounded like the truth. Brian liked to drink, but he rarely did so to excess when I was around. What was pissing me off the most was how he treated me and Sam. "I knew we were having problems, but I never knew he was lying to me, trying to pick up strange men, and..."

"I'm not strange." Cary winked, and something in my heart burst. The man I'd trusted my family and career with had lied to me, repeatedly, I bet.

"Oh baby, I'm so sorry." Cary said, and a sob tore through me. I leaned against him, feeling my shoulders quake as tears streamed down my face. He placed his arm over my shoulders and pulled me into his chest. "It's going to be alright, I swear it will, Thatch. I'll make it right, I promise."

————

"What am I going to do?" I swiped at my eyes. "Brian is so intertwined in my life. I own homes with him, and he manages my finances. What if he's been doing other shady stuff, too?"

Cary patted me on the knee and stood up. "First, I need a drink. Do you want one too?"

"Yeah, beer, in the mini-fridge over there." I pointed at the kitchen.

"I can tell you what I would do, but ultimately you have to decide what you want to do about your husband." Cary pulled two beers from the fridge and walked back over to the couch.

"My ex-husband." I corrected him, and took a beer and opened it.

"Well, in many ways, he's still your spouse." Cary held his hand up. "Hear me out. You own two or three homes together, and his income is solely derived from you, unless he represents other authors."

"I think he reps a couple of other writers, but none of them..."

"... make what you make." Cary finished my sentence. "First, I'd give him the benefit of the doubt and have an audit performed. If he's done nothing crooked, he won't object. If he objects, I have the best accountants in the world on my payroll, and the best lawyers." Cary leaned back and placed his index finger on his chin for a moment. "I hate to tell you this, but it could be like divorcing him all over again. It might even end up in court, depending on the contracts you've signed."

"Shit." I muttered, then drained the beer. "What about Sam?"

"Sam is an adult. He can take care of himself. Yes, he might be upset if you and Brian end up duking it out through the legal system, but he's a big boy. I'm more worried about something else."

"What?" I got to my feet to get another beer out of the fridge, but Cary's words stopped me in my tracks.

"Are you still in love with Brian?"

CHAPTER 29
CARY

"No. Cary, I haven't felt true love for Brian in years." Thatch's voice trembled, and I wanted nothing more than to take him in my arms and kiss his pain away. I wasn't sure what was happening to me, but I was certain of one thing. Thatch had awakened feelings that I'd never had for anyone else, but I had to know if he was even able to consider exploring them with me first.

"Old habits die hard, don't they?" I murmured as Thatch strolled into the kitchen for another beer.

"What did you say?" Thatch asked while rummaging in the fridge. To my relief, he came back with a bottle of coke instead of beer. Emotional drinking rarely made the bad stuff go away. It mostly prolonged the agony.

"Brian is like an addiction, isn't he?"

Thatch sat next to me and opened the bottle of soda. "I'm not sure what you mean, but we have been in each other's lives for decades. Brian takes care of all the stuff I hate dealing with, like publishing crap. He also pays the bills, arranges trips, well, he's kind of like my Jenny."

"There's a vast difference between Jenny and Brian. First of all, Jenny isn't my accountant, and I've never had an intimate relationship with her, much less a child. Do I trust her? Yes. She's never taken advantage of me, does an outstanding job, and I pay her very well for her services." I leaned back into the cushions and draped an arm over Thatch's shoulders. "She's a friend as well as an employee, but I maintain certain boundaries with her."

"Well, as far as I know, Brian hasn't done anything unethical, and he's Sam's Dad. As far as I'm concerned, he's innocent until proven guilty." Thatch's gaze met mine and I rubbed the back of his neck. "But, maybe it's time to cut the cord. Mixing personal and business relationships isn't for the best. I've always known that, but figured Brian and I were the exception to that rule."

"I will support whatever you decide to do, but I must confess that when you said you weren't in love with him, it made my heart skip a beat." The words poured out of my mouth before my inner censor could stop me. Thatch froze, and I held my breath, waiting for him to respond. Finally, he turned to me, and brushed his lips over mine.

"Thank you."

"For what?" I whispered.

"Being you. When we first met, I thought you were a sketchy playboy, trying to take advantage of my son. Now I know you have a huge heart, and whenever I think of you, something inside me smiles." Thatch stood up, and held his hand out for me to take.

"What happens next?" I asked, and Thatch pulled me to my feet.

"I don't know, but I'm hoping that whatever it is, you are with me."

———

After lunch, Thatch returned to his office to make phone calls, and I cleaned up the mess in Sam's room the best I could. I tossed the leaves and branches out the broken windows, and disposed of the broken glass. But, I was no housekeeper, and I hoped Thatch would allow me to get Jenny involved. She could literally have a cleaning crew here in a matter of hours.

Despite the wonderful night we'd spent together, I wasn't sure how to move things forward with Thatch. I believed him when he said he wasn't in love with his ex-husband, but that didn't mean there wasn't a... damn it, what was that overused word again?

"Codependency. That's it." I muttered, then pulled my phone out and sent Thatch a text letting him know I would be in the game room. I loved shooting pool, and pinball was fun too. Since Thatch hadn't asked me for help, I thought I'd indulge in a little fun now, since this place would be overrun with maids, landscapers, and contractors soon.

I'd gotten used to the stairs leading to the bedrooms, but the stairs going to the basement were more difficult. The light was dimmer, and there wasn't a railing, so I held on to the wall as I descended the stairs. When I got to the bottom my phone buzzed, so I pulled it out and saw a message from Thatch.

Be there in a few minutes

When I stepped into the basement I felt water seep into my loafers. "Yuck."

I flipped on the lights and began setting up for a pool match, assuming that Thatch knew how to play. That's when it struck me that there was a chance that Brian had been gaslighting Thatch for years, and he was so accustomed to it that he couldn't see Brian's bad behavior for what it really was.

A way of controlling Thatch, and keeping his pockets full of money.

"But I can't say anything to him, because he might think I'm interfering, sticking my nose where it doesn't belong." I sighed, then chose a pool stick and began chalking it up. There was no way this thing Thatch and I had just started could go much further if what I believed about Brian was true. Brain would sabotage us, and Thatch wouldn't even know it was happening. Or, worse, he'd know it, but feel powerless to do anything. He had to tackle this problem himself, and all I could do was be there for him as a friend, or hopefully, something deeper.

"Hey baby," Thatch called from the top of the stairs. A moment later he pecked me on the cheek and grabbed a pool stick.

"You any good?" I gestured toward the table.

"I used to be," Thatch said, "...but it's been a while since I played last, so you might have a chance."

"Sounds like a challenge." I winked. "Go ahead, you break."

"I called my landscapers, and you were right. They can't be here for another two weeks, and the same goes for my cleaning service." Thatch lined up the cue ball and made his first shot. It was a perfect break, and the nine ball dropped into the corner pocket. His next shot accidentally sank the cue ball.

"I'll call Jenny. She'll have workers here in the morning, most likely. You're probably going to need contractors too, especially for the insurance claims." I aimed for the two ball, and it narrowly missed the side pocket. "Shit." I muttered. "Out of practice."

Thatch slowly walked around the table, then aimed for the seven ball. "Thank you, Cary. Can I ask another favor?"

"Sure."

He sank the seven ball, then took a deep breath and spoke.

"Your accountants. Are they your employees, or are they just people you hire from a firm?"

"A firm. They are completely independent from me, and I prefer it that way. If I signed their paycheck they would give me biased information. The name of the firm is Dallin, Woodward, and Fahey. They've been around since the Earth cooled, and my parents used them too."

"Can you give me their contact information? I spent a lot of time in my office trying to piece together my financial picture, and I'll admit to being too much an artist. Numbers confuse me, and I've decided to go ahead with an audit." Thatch leaned over, eyed the five ball, and sank it in a corner pocket. "I should probably find an entertainment lawyer while I'm at it. Someone familiar with publishing."

There was a flutter in my belly, and I did my best not to jump up and down and scream, yes, Thatch, do it! But, I bit my lip instead, not wanting to come across as too excited. "I don't deal with this stuff much, myself. Why don't I have Jenny come here tomorrow. Might as well, since there's going to be a ton of people here for the next few days."

Thatch laid his pool stick on the table, knocking a few balls in at the same time, then came around the table to where I was standing. "I'm going to hate having people here. It means I can't be alone with you very much."

I wrapped my hands around his neck and pulled him in for a kiss. What started out as a simple kiss deepened, and I felt my cock firming up at his touch. My heart was pounding so fast that if Dr. Creighton had been here she would've called an ambulance. Finally, I broke the kiss, and breathlessly asked, "Here on the pool table, or your bedroom?"

CHAPTER 30

CARY

"Good morning." Thatch's deep voice rumbled. He was holding me tight against his chest, his entire body molded to mine.

"Morning, handsome. Sleep well?"

I felt him move behind me and realized he was glancing at the clock on the nightstand. "We've slept for almost nine hours. Swear to God, Cary, you're better than a sleeping pill."

"I haven't slept this well since I was a teenager." I yawned. "Jenny said she'd be here bright and early with the cleaning team. We're putting them up in a hotel close by. The landscapers are expected soon after that."

"When you said she could get anything done quickly and efficiently, you weren't lying." Thatch murmured, then kissed the back of my neck. My skin pebbled at his touch, and I wished we could stay in bed just a little longer.

"Hand me my phone, please." I asked. Thatch gave it to me and I checked my messages. "Jenny texted an hour ago from some town named Greensboro. She said she'd be here by ten, so we'd better get ready. We've got to meet them at the gate since the driveway is still impassable." I turned, so I was lying flat on my back.

"Damn it." Thatch grumbled. "Can't we just pretend that everything is working perfectly, that the storm never happened?"

"I wish, big boy." I reached down and squeezed my morning wood. "Trust me, there's nothing I would love better than to stay in bed and make love to you."

Thatch rolled on top of me and grinned, then kissed the tip of my nose. I could feel his erection, and wondered if perhaps Jenny and the cleaners wouldn't mind waiting a little while longer at the gate.

"C'mon. We've got a lot going on today, and both of us need a shower." Thatch rolled off of me and got out of bed. "Would you mind using the guest room's bathroom? Because, if we take a shower together, Jenny will be waiting for a very long time."

———

Thatch wanted to make food for everyone, but I told him to wait. Though I was feeling much better, I knew I didn't have the strength to hike all the way down the driveway to meet them. So, Thatch went alone, and while he was gone, I searched the pantry for paper plates, disposable utensils, and snacks that didn't require any cooking. What I secretly hoped for was that we could rope one of the abuelas into cooking.

"There is a layer of dust covering your Rolls Royce."

Jenny startled me, and I dropped a bag of chips on the floor. "Jesus, you scared me."

A second later, she was hugging me tight, and she whispered in my ear. "Something is going on with you and the hot writer, I can tell. Usually you share everything with me, but lately you've been a bit cagey."

Before I could answer, Thatch stepped into the kitchen, followed by five older latinas. I eyed them, and said, "Hello, my name is Cary. Would one of you like to work in the kitchen today?"

"No, Cary, I can feed everyone." Thatch grinned, but I shook my head no.

"You know this house better than anyone, so you need to supervise. Plus, I bet one of these ladies would enjoy cooking." I grinned at the women, and one of them stepped forward.

"I would love to work in the kitchen. My name is Elisa." She was a short woman with a full head of gray hair with a slight blue tint to it. "Should I start with a light breakfast, or prepare lunch?"

"We're going to be working hard today, so let's eat a little something before we get to work. A light breakfast would be perfect." Jenny glanced down at her watch. "Mr. Fuller, would you mind showing the ladies around the house so we know what we're dealing with? I need to hustle back to the gate to meet the landscapers. I'll bring them up here, so they can grab a bite, too."

And just like that, the romantic bubble Thatch and I had been living in was popped.

Jenny thrust a leather bag in my hand, and from its weight I knew it had a laptop inside, and papers to be signed. The woman named Elisa wrapped an apron around her waist and sneered at the snacks I'd laid out. Thatch left to give the other cleaning women the tour, and I immediately felt useless.

"Does Mr. Fuller have tortillas?" Elisa asked, and I shrugged my shoulders, then pointed at the pantry door, and she went inside. A moment later, she came out with a huge smile on her face. "Mr. Fuller must love Mexicano food. He has the best pantry I've ever seen, well, except for my Mama's."

Her accent was thick, and I had difficulty understanding her, so I nodded and felt stupid.

"Oh, he even has a comal. It's a good one too." She pulled out what appeared to be a flat, cast-iron griddle and set it on the stove. Then she piled tortillas on it, and the room began to smell like corn.

A sense of loss weighed down on my shoulders. All of this activity, the abuelas, and the landscapers, even the presence of Jenny, meant this romantic dream was coming to an end. In the past, I would've graciously bowed out and moved on to my next amorous adventure. But now I felt unsure. Would Thatch still want to see me after the dust had settled?

Since the woman cooking was busy, and I couldn't be of any use to her, I strolled into the living room to see what Jenny had brought me. After sitting down, I opened the leather bag and tried to work, but I struggled to focus. All I could think about was that somehow I had changed. When I'd first arrived here, all I wanted was to tap Sam's ass for the first time, then we probably would've kept seeing each other for a few weeks, until either I or Sam grew bored and moved on.

What was it about Thatcher Atticus Fuller? He stirred feelings in me I'd never had before. Was it my near-death experience, or was this meant to be, like one of those cheesy Hallmark movies I couldn't bear to watch?

I'd always considered myself a romantic, but with very specific boundaries. Rarely, if ever, did I have sleepovers with the men I'd dated. But, with Thatch, I was getting the best sleep of my life. I'd always thought monogamy was silly. Like, who was I to tell someone who they could or couldn't sleep with? But now, the thought of touching anyone else sexually held no appeal.

"Swear to God if I walked in on him with another guy, I'd blow a gasket." I whispered, shaking my head in wonder. I'd completely changed in a matter of days, and honestly, I wondered if I should…

"… and the contractors need to look at the basement first before you will clean it. Otherwise, you can get to work right after we eat." Thatch said as he came down the stairs, the cleaners walking in single file behind him. "Getting some work done, Cary?" He strolled over and placed his hand on the back of my neck and smiled, and my stomach flipped at his touch.

"Ladies, grab a bite to eat, and then you can get to work." Thatch said, then sat down next to me as the women went to the kitchen. "I can't wait for all this crap to be done. Having all these people in my house is making me crazy."

"Even me?" I murmured coyly, then realized I was now talking like a character in one of those romantic films.

"Of course not. You're not allowed to leave yet." Thatch said, then a red flush crept up his neck. "Shit, I didn't mean to…"

"You're fine, Thatch, I promise." I turned and kissed his cheek.

"And we're getting more visitors tomorrow." He sighed, and I raised an eyebrow. "While showing the ladies around, I got a bunch of text messages."

"Who? Why would anyone come here when you're having all this work done?"

"Celia Mae and Sam insist on coming, so they'll be here later this afternoon." Thatch sighed, then grimaced.

"What aren't you telling me?" I asked and rubbed his knee. Thatch took a deep breath and frowned.

"Brian is coming too."

CHAPTER 31

THATCH

"What?" Cary cocked an eyebrow. "Brian's coming? You've got to be kidding me."

"I tried telling him that this was a bad time, but he insisted on seeing the property damage in person." I sighed and shook my head. "But, I'm sure he's also coming to give me an earful about you. Why the hell does he even care who I date?"

A soft glow colored Cary's cheeks. "So we're officially dating now?"

"What else would you call it?" I murmured, then I placed my hand on the back of his neck and pulled him in for a kiss.

"I knew it." Jenny's voice stopped me, and both Cary and I turned in her direction. "And I definitely approve, boss." She strolled over to us and handed me a folder. "Cary asked me to get you the contact info for the accounting firm we use, and I made a list of reputable entertainment lawyers and agents. If I were you, I'd check out the William Morris agency first. If you want your books turned into movies, they're the best."

"Thanks," I muttered, and a bolt of fear tore through me.

Brian had always handled these things for me, and now I was about to take back control of my career. Hell, I was taking back control of my life. "Jesus, this would be so much easier to do over a video call."

"I'm sorry, I didn't get that." Jenny sat across from us on the white leather loveseat.

"Brian, Thatch's ex-husband is coming. He's also his literary agent and handles much of Thatch's finances. That's why I asked you for this information, so he could get..." Cary began, but I cut him off.

"Answers. I need to know if Brian has been honest with me about, well, everything."

"Okay." Jenny's gaze floated between me and Cary, and her brow furrowed. "Cary, when you have a free moment, I would love to touch base with you about something important. Mr. Fuller, I forgot to tell you that the landscapers are here. I offered them food, but they'd already eaten. They are clearing the driveway before they do anything else, so any visitors should be able to get to the house without a problem."

"Thanks, and please, call me Thatch." I got to my feet and glanced at my watch. "We still have a few hours before my family shows up. I'd better get to work."

———

"Cary, it's wonderful to see you again." Celia Mae air kissed him on both cheeks, while I marveled at her changed attitude toward him. "You are looking much better. Wonder why?" She winked and hugged me.

"Looking good, Cary." Sam hugged him, then he stood in front of me and put his hands on his hips. "He'd better be sleeping in your room."

"Jesus, kid. Stop it." Cary muttered, and his cheeks grew

pinker, then a shy smile, one I'd never seen him make before, split his face. "Your room is a disaster, by the way. The storm hit it pretty hard."

Sam was about to reply, but I spoke before he could. "Celia Mae, Sam, Cary, I need to speak with y'all in private. Let's go upstairs to my office."

My sister's mouth hit the floor. "You're actually letting us into your secret writing cave?"

I forced myself to smile. "C'mon. This is important." I gestured toward the stairs, and the three of them went up, with me following behind them.

My son kept glancing back at me, probably wondering what I meant to share with them. He had to know it was serious, and assuming Brian had told him he was on his way, he probably knew it had something to do with him. It did, but more importantly, it was about me.

Celia Mae opened the door and stepped inside. "Wow, Thatch, the storm didn't hurt this room at all." She strolled around it for a moment, then sat down on the couch, with Sam and Cary settling next to her. I perched on the edge of my desk and sighed.

"So, what I'm about to share might shock you." I said, then cleared my throat. "I'm ending my business arrangements with Brian, and I intend on either buying out his share of our real estate holdings, or forcing a sale of the three properties."

Sam's face scrunched up, and I prayed he wouldn't cry. I'd spent years trying to keep my relationship with Brian healthy, so Sam wouldn't ever feel like he had to choose between us.

"It's about damned time," Celia Mae patted Sam on the knee and stood up. "You have any booze here?" She strolled over to the mini-kitchen and started rummaging through the cabinets.

"Beer in the fridge, and liquor is in the—"

"Found it." She pulled a bottle of beer out of the fridge and twisted off the top. "Anyone else?"

We all shook our heads no.

"Thatch, you're my big brother and I love you, but when you divorce someone, you need to move on with your entire life. Instead, you've held on to the bitter end trying to make things work out with Brian." She sipped her beer and grinned. "Honey, it's time to cut the cord. And Sam, I know this might be hard to hear, but both your Dads need to get on with their lives. It doesn't mean Thatch doesn't love you if he goes his own way."

"Jesus, it almost feels like you're getting divorced all over again." Sam muttered. "Dad, you do what's best for you. I'm an adult, and while I don't know much about you and my other dad's business stuff, I just want you to be happy." Sam hooked a thumb in Cary's direction. "Does this have anything to do with him?"

A flush raced up Cary's neck. "This is all your father's doing, Sam. I have nothing to do with it."

"Cary has, shit. What's the right word?" I tapped the side of my nose. "Cary helped me make my decision, but it was all mine to make." Sam started to say something, but I held my hand up. "I'm not saying anything bad about Brian to you, Sam. And for the record, I want to be friends with Brian for your sake. The only way that will happen is if we untangle our lives from one another. That means he won't be my agent any longer, and we won't have any more financial dealings with each other."

"I don't understand." Sam tilted his head. "What does him being your agent have to do with anything?"

Shit. How could I explain that I doubted Brian had my best interests at heart? I didn't have proof he was doing anything shady, well, except for the lie about Cary coming on to him, and

I didn't want Sam to even know about that stuff. It wasn't any of his business. Brian had always been a good father to Sam, and I wasn't about to hurt their relationship.

"Sam," I chose my words with care. "It's time for me to be truly on my own, and I can't do that if my life and Brian's life are so enmeshed with each other."

"You think he's ripping you off?" Celia Mae sat down next to Sam and I shot her a look. My sister often spoke without thinking and now wasn't the time for her to keep flapping her gums.

"Celia Mae, if you could.." There was a knock at the door, and I assumed it was Jenny, or one of the cleaners. "Give me a moment."

I walked to the door and opened it. Brian was standing there with his arms crossed over his chest.

"Brian. I knew you were coming, but..."

"You let everyone into your office except me, apparently." He stalked past me, hitting my shoulder with his as he did. Brian looked heavier, and I could see a thin line of gray hair coming from his scalp. He needed to retouch his roots. "What the hell is he still doing here?" Brian pointed at Cary, who looked like he wanted to be anywhere but in my office.

"I invited him, unlike you." I snapped and instantly regretted it. Fighting with Brian in front of Sam was a definite no-no.

"I own half this house and I will come and go as I please." Brian said, then had the balls to sit behind my desk. When he did, I noticed the folder Jenny had given me in front of him, filled with the names of other agents, lawyers, and accountants.

"If you choose to be surly, trust me, Brian, I will hit back harder." I growled and again regretted it. Glancing over to Sam, I saw his eyes were wet. Throughout our relationship, both Brian and I took pains not to fight in front of our son.

"You and I have always had a cordial relationship, but something has changed." Brian put his feet on top of my desk, and without thinking, I walked over and knocked them off. His hazel eyes squinted, and I couldn't tell if he was pissed off, or intimidated by my action.

"Boys, calm down." I turned at the sound of my sister's voice. "Whatever needs to be spoken about can be said without acting like two bulls fighting over a cow."

Cary's eyes met mine, and I wished it was just me and him, alone. I turned back to Brian and struggled to keep my voice even.

"Celia Mae's right. I can say what I have to say without getting nasty, and I expect the same from you, Brian."

He shrugged his shoulders, then I grabbed the folder off the desk.

"I'm having my financial records audited by an independent accounting firm, and then I'm finding a new agent."

Brian's eyes widened, and he hit the desk with his fist. "The hell you will. We built your career together. I was there when you were nothing, working crappy jobs when not a single publisher would touch you. How dare you...?"

"Enough!" Cary yelled. "Jesus Christ, act like civilized human beings." Cary got to his feet and glared at Brian. "This is business, that's all. And Thatch has every right under the law to conduct it as he sees fit."

Celia Mae tugged on his sleeve, and he sat down. Sam patted him on the knee, then spoke. "I hate seeing you argue, but Dad..." he pointed at Brian, "... maybe it's time for you guys to go your separate ways."

"I will not see my life's work go down the drain because, well, because of you." Brian pointed at Cary. "You're screwing Thatch, aren't you?"

Cary's cheeks flushed, but he said nothing.

"It's not Cary's fault you lied about him coming on to you. That's all your doing." I crossed my arms over my chest and glared down at him.

"You believe that scum?" Brian threw his hands in the air and looked at me like I was a total idiot, and I was, for believing him all these years.

"What the hell?" Sam stood up. "Cary would never have come on to you, Dad. You're too old."

Brian's mouth opened, then shut.

"I can't believe you are lying to all of us. Jesus, Brian." Sam said, and my heart sank. He sounded so sad. Plus, he'd never called either of us by our first name. "Why would you come up with a crazy story like that? And why would you want to?"

Brian jumped to his feet and pointed at Cary.

"If I'm too old, why is he fucking Thatch?"

"I'm in love with him." Cary and I spoke at the same time, and everyone gasped. I turned to Cary, a feeling of wonder spreading through my limbs.

"Are you really in love with me?" Cary asked, his voice trembling. He rose and crossed over to me, opening his arms. "Because, I'm not lying, and I'll never, ever lie to you. You've made me a better man, and I truly, truly, love you."

I stepped into his embrace and felt tears sliding down my cheeks. "Oh my God, I never thought I could feel this way again. I love you, Cary, I…"

I couldn't finish my sentence, because Brian grabbed me from behind and yanked me out of Cary's arms.

"Get the fuck out of my house!"

CHAPTER 32

CARY

People thought I was a powerful person. Some would even say I was intimidating, but when physical violence entered the picture, I would bolt through the nearest exit, and wait for the dust to settle. This was different though, because Thatch was being threatened by his asshole ex-husband, and I was seeing red.

"Brian, what the hell are you thinking?" Celia Mae's voice rang out. Then she sprang from her seat, grabbed him by the shoulders, and pushed him away from me and Thatch. "You've gone too far." She stuck her finger in his face, and shouted, "You lay one hand on either Thatch or Cary and God help me, I will snatch you bald!"

Brian raised his fist and Sam leapt to his aunt's side. "Brian, sit your ass down!"

He froze, staring at Sam like he was just seeing him for the first time. "You called me by my name." He mumbled, then dropped his fist and turned to go sit behind Thatch's desk.

"Do not sit at my desk." Thatch's voice boomed. Brian stared at him, and for the first time, I felt pity for the man.

These people were once his family, and now they wanted to cut him off, or at least that was what I suspected he felt like they were doing. What must it be like to feel betrayed by the people he used to count on most? Of course, like most foolish people, he'd brought it on himself and like most foolish men, he was probably going to make things worse.

Brian inhaled, then held his hands up in mock surrender. "Let's talk this through rationally." He turned and sat on the couch.

Celia Mae refused to sit next to Brian, preferring to glare at him while she paced the length of the room. Sam sat next to him, keeping several inches between the two of them, while Thatch sat behind his desk. Me? I leaned against the wall by the door in case I needed to make a quick getaway. Also, this was a family affair. I might have told Thatch that I loved him for the first time, but ultimately, I wasn't involved. This was between two ex-husbands who'd never completely let go of each other.

Thatch steepled his hands under his chin and quietly spoke. "You helped me tremendously when my career started. Now, I've decided to go in another direction. I want a new literary agent, and I want to sever all financial ties with you."

Brian started to speak, but Celia Mae yelled, "Hush your mouth!"

"This will include our shared real estate holdings. I was considering giving you the apartment in New York in exchange for this house, and we'd sell the home in Nags Head, but I think a clean break is in my best interest. I want all three properties sold, and we will each keep fifty percent of the proceeds." Thatch's lips flattened for a moment, and a chill went up my spine. I'd only seen the creative and kind side of Thatch. Now I was seeing a calculated businessman, and I respected the hell out of him.

"What if I don't want to sell? I could easily take you to

court, and though I won't win, I can keep you tied up in litiga-
tion for years." Brian thrust his chin out. "It would be worth
every damned penny."

"If you do that, I'll never see or speak to you again, Brian."
Sam glared at him, and Brian winced. "Why did you lie about
Cary?"

Brian shook his head, his lips twisting at the same time.
"He's a conceited asshole who..."

"...rejected your advances. Your ego can't stand it." Thatch
pursed his lips. "Everyone gets turned down occasionally, so I
don't buy what you're selling. There's more to this story than
you're letting on."

"Cary, what the hell did you do to Brian?" Celia Mae asked,
then blew a blonde lock off of her forehead. "He's like a banty
rooster, trying to... oh my God." She winked at Brian. "Bless
your heart, dickhead, I know what it is." She glanced back at
me. "Sugar, you've got nothing to do with this."

I shrugged my shoulders, holding my hands up in the air.
"I'm leaving."

"No, you don't..." Thatch began, but I cut him off.

"Yes, I must." I strolled over to the desk and kissed Thatch
on the cheek. "This is about you, your ex, and your family." I
faced all of them and took a deep breath. "I wish you all the
best of luck, but I'm an outsider. This is family business, so I'll
leave you to it." I squeezed Thatch's shoulders, then walked to
the door. "And Brian, do the right thing and finish what you
guys started when you divorced each other."

———

I marched to Sam's room and was about to shut the door when
I noticed someone was in the bathroom. It was one of the
cleaners.

"Excuse me, would you mind working in another part of the house for a few minutes?"

The woman nodded, and seconds later, she was out the door. She had stripped the bed of sheets and blankets, so I didn't worry about accidentally cutting myself on broken glass. I sat down and sighed. Like Celia Mae, I was pretty sure of what was happening with Thatch and Brian. I seriously doubted he'd been embezzling money, or anything else shady. He just wanted to be in control of everything, including his ex-husband. I was a threat, because I represented freedom for Thatch, and after decades of controlling his ex, Brian had to move on without him. There was a lot of money involved, but he could probably retire on the proceeds from the sale of the three properties alone.

"Knock knock."

I glanced up to see Jenny's sharp gaze. "Are they still fighting? You can hear it all the way down in the kitchen."

I nodded and gestured for her to enter. "After all these years, they're finally breaking up."

"Oh dear." Jenny sat next to me and laid her head on my shoulder. "You're in love with hot-writer guy, aren't you?"

"Oh yes." I grinned, but then the true reality of the situation settled onto my shoulders. "Until he cuts himself off from his ex-husband, we can't take things any further. My hunch was right. They are totally codependent on each other."

"You can still go out with him, you know, support him while he's going through the divo... oh yeah, they already are divorced."

We both shook our heads and chuckled.

"I have no problem dating Thatch while he's going through this, but right now I feel like my presence isn't helping. As much as I want to be here with Thatch, I need to leave, so he can figure things out with Brian." I said, then heard muffled screaming and what sounded like glass breaking. My shoulders stiffened, and both of us sat up straight. "Hopefully, they won't inflict permanent damage."

"Jesus, there's a lot of anger between the two of them." Jenny muttered, then the door flew open. Thatch stood there, tears streaking his cheeks. I leapt to my feet.

"Cary, I'm so sorry."

I opened my arms and Thatch stepped into them, wrapping his arms around my shoulders. Out of the corner of my eye, I saw Jenny sneak out, a pained look on her normally cheery face.

"There's nothing for you to be sorry about. Thatch, I love you. I truly do." I let go of him and gestured toward the mattress. "Sit with me for a moment." We sat down, and I took his hand in mine and squeezed it. "You've got a lot of stuff on your plate right now, and you might not enjoy hearing this, but I'm going back to Raleigh."

"No, please, I…"

"I'm only a phone call away, and I'll see a doctor as soon as possible. But what you are dealing with is…"

"Celia Mae was right." Thatch sniffed. "Brian isn't furious about you. He's angry about losing the privileged life we built together. He's afraid of being humiliated, and that he'll lose everything."

"Is everyone safe? Because Jenny and I heard more screaming and glass breaking." I rubbed his back and felt a tiny sob vibrate inside him.

"That was my sister. She threw a beer bottle at Brian when he called her a dried-up crone who lived vicariously through my career." Thatch swiped at his eyes. "It actually hit his leg, then broke on the floor. That's when I ran out of the room. I hope my sister's okay."

"I wouldn't want to piss off Celia Mae." I bit my lip to keep from giggling. Thatch turned to me and smiled, then ruffled my hair.

"It's best that you leave, though I wish you wouldn't." He brushed his lips across mine, and despite the seriousness of the situation, I swooned. "Brian and I had the most civilized of divorces, all for Sam's sake. Now, we're speaking and feeling all the horrible shit we were too dignified to say at the time."

"I'm so sorry, babe. If I could take away this pain, I would." A tear spilled down my cheek. I wanted nothing more than to be here for him, but if I stayed, I'd probably trigger some sort of drama with Brian.

"Can you do me a huge favor?" Thatch kissed the tip of my nose, and his wet, blue eyes locked with mine.

"Anything."

"Take Sam with you. He doesn't need to go through this hell, too."

CHAPTER 33

THATCH

When Cary and I returned to my office, Brian wasn't there. A chill went up my spine, because I didn't trust him wandering around alone in our house.

"Celia Mae, where did Brian go?"

"He just left a minute ago. Probably went to the bathroom. Who knows?" She grimaced, then tugged at a large wooden bracelet on her wrist. "I'm wound up tighter than a girdle at a baptist potluck."

Cary and Sam snickered.

"Sam, Cary is leaving for Raleigh, and I'd like you to go with him. He'll drop you off in Chapel Hill on the way." He was seated on the couch, staring at his phone. Sam shifted his gaze to Cary, then to me.

"Are you sure that's a good idea? Has the doctor cleared him to leave?"

"Honest to God, Cary is safer leaving than staying. Brian is in jackass mode, and he's making me nervous, too." Celia Mae clucked her tongue, then looped her arm through mine. "Maybe you should go too, Thatch. He's not acting right."

"I've always wanted to say this to your face." Brian's voice growled from behind us, and we all spun around to stare at him in the doorway. "Celia Mae, when God made bitches, you were his inspiration." His eyes were squinty, and his hands were balled into fists. "And you," Brian glowered at Cary. "Why are you hell-bent on destroying everything I've worked for?"

"Brian!" Sam got up from the couch and placed his arm around his aunt. "What is wrong with you? I was going to stay, but now I'm taking off with Cary. You need to chill, smoke a joint or something. I realize you hate what's happening, but you can't just…"

"You're right." Brian cut him off, holding his hands in the air. "Maybe I just need to let off a little steam." He turned and jogged toward the stairs.

Nobody said a word for a few moments. Honestly, I couldn't figure out why Brian was so upset about Cary. Our marriage had been over for years, and I didn't know if he was jealous of him, or believed that Cary was the instigator for my ending our business arrangements. If he did, he was giving me little credit for making my own decisions.

"Dad, if you don't mind, I want to hit the road. Watching my other dad act like a mental patient who's escaped from an institution isn't exactly my idea of fun." Sam walked over to Cary and put his arm over his shoulder. "Will you let me drive? At least for a little while? This might be my only chance to get behind the wheel of a Rolls Royce."

Cary grinned. "No problem, Sam. Let's hit the road."

"Yes!" Sam jumped up and down, and despite his age, he reminded me of his teenage years.

"Thatch, I don't trust you being alone with Brian. He's liable to do something crazy." Celia Mae said, then a loud scream came from downstairs.

"Jenny!" Cary took off for the stairs, with the rest of us behind him.

"Oh my God! No!" A feminine voice screamed, then a chorus of them began shrieking. By now, Cary was halfway down the stairs. I could see the entrance to the garage was open, and sharp clanging sounds were coming through. Cary stopped in his tracks and grabbed his chest, gasping for air.

"Babe, are you okay?" I went to grab for him but he held his hand up. Sam and Celia Mae ran down the stairs ahead of us.

"I knew that fucker was up to no good." Celia Mae called out. "Sam, the garage!"

"Yeah, just, hard to breathe." Cary stood up straight, and in moments his breathing slowed to normal. "Thatch, promise me something."

"Anything." I pulled him into my chest and felt his heart pounding against mine.

Cary glanced up at me and struggled to smile. "Don't over-react. If Brian is doing something crazy, which is virtually guaranteed, don't give him what he wants. It will be playing into his hands."

A blood-curdling scream came from the garage, and Cary's face paled.

"Can you make it?" Jesus, nothing I'd ever been through prepared me for this drama.

Cary nodded, and I placed my hand on the small of his back and we hurried down the stairs. When we entered the hallway leading to the garage, I heard Brian screech.

"Get off me, you fucking bitch!"

"Oh shit, Jenny!" Cary jogged ahead of me, and I was terrified he'd collapse. But when we entered the garage, we both froze in our tracks.

Brian was brandishing the poker from the fireplace and had been smashing up Cary's Rolls Royce. Glass was everywhere, and Jenny was on Brian's back, screaming. The maids were cowering against the far wall crying, and I saw the landscape crew through the tiny windows yelling and holding their phones up, videotaping the destruction.

Sam whipped out his phone and started recording. "Aunt Celia Mae, open the garage door!"

My sister grabbed her keys out of her pocket, then instantly dropped them and picked them up again. She pushed the door opener on her fob and the door slowly rose.

"You fucking cunt!" Brian screamed and I saw his ear between Jenny's teeth. With a bellow, he backed into the wall, pinning her behind him. She let go of his ear, and Celia Mae strolled over and kicked him in the nuts with her high-heel boots. He swung at her with the fire poker, then dropped it and fell to the floor with his hands clutching his junk. Jenny cackled, then kicked him in the gut.

"Don't fuck with me, you scummy piece of shit!!" Jenny lifted her leg to kick him again, and I saw Celia Mae about to do the same.

"Stop!" Cary yelled. "For the love of God, stop!"

Everyone froze.

"But your car, it's..." Jenny began, but Cary cut her off.

"It's a car, that's all. I have insurance, and I can afford another one. What's important is that nobody gets hurt." Cary walked over to Brian and reached a hand down to help him up.

Brian spat on him. "I hate you." He muttered through clenched teeth.

"Welcome to the club. You're not the first to say that." Cary straightened up, wiping his hand on his pants. "Jenny, would you get your car please? We're leaving. The cleaning team must get out of here, and the landscapers too." Despite his calm words, his voice was trembling, and when he turned to me, I saw tears in his eyes. "Thatch, you and Celia Mae can't stay here. It's not safe while your ex-husband is, you know." He gestured toward Brian, who was attempting to get to his feet. The poker was inches away from him, and Celia Mae stepped forward and kicked it out of his reach. Then Jenny kicked him in the ribs and he sank back to the floor.

"Don't fuck with strong women, asshole." Jenny grunted.

"Cary, we need to call the police." I sighed, then pulled him into my arms.

"I already did." One of the landscapers yelled. "They'll be here any minute. We got most of it on video."

"I don't want to prosecute him." Cary sighed, shaking his head. "He's going through hell because…"

"Fuck that shit, Cary. He's already broken numerous laws, including threatening the maids. When they tried to stop him, he attacked them with the poker. That's why they're all crying." Jenny pointed at them.

Sirens could be heard in the distance, and I glanced down and saw tears streaming from Brian's bloodshot eyes. In all the decades I'd known him, I'd never seen him fall apart like this. That's when I saw a tiny plastic bag next to him on the ground. It was filled with something white, like a powder.

"Is that what I think it is?" I whispered in Cary's ear and pointed. His eyebrows pointed toward the ceiling, and Jenny must have noticed it at the same time. She reached down to pick it up, but I stopped her.

"Don't." I shook my head. "Let the police handle this, plus you don't want your fingerprints on it."

Brian obviously wasn't deaf, and he frantically searched the ground around him before finding the baggie and thrusting it back into his pocket. Then he pointed his finger at all of us and said, "If any of you say a word about this, I'll kill you."

Smiles spread across Celia Mae's and Jenny's cheeks. Celia Mae winked at him and cooed, "Bless your heart, Brian."

———

Hours later, my former husband was behind bars and the only people left at the house were me, Cary, my sister, Sam, and Jenny. A half-empty bottle of tequila was on the kitchen counter, and we were on the verge of finishing up all the beer in the fridge.

"What I don't get is why Brian lost it so bad." Celia Mae said, then poured a shot of tequila down her throat and bit into a lime. "I used to love that man like a brother, and he just…"

"New York has that effect on some people." Cary squeezed my hand, which was resting in his lap. "You get invited to certain parties and suddenly you develop a nasty little cocaine habit. I hated the stuff, found it boring. And Thatch?"

I nodded and tilted my head.

"You must get your audit done ASAP. He was likely frantic, because he was running out of cash, and he suspected his primary money maker was about to leave him high and dry."

"Oh shit." Sam muttered, then handed Celia Mae his phone. "Look at this."

She stared at the screen for a moment, handed me the phone, and poured herself another shot.

"Another one," I sighed and showed Cary the screen. This was the seventh video we'd seen on social media of Brian laying waste to Cary's Rolls Royce. The landscapers had filmed almost the entire encounter since they'd been outside the garage, taking a smoke break when he'd begun. They'd heard the screams of the maids and started filming through the windows. The bastards hadn't even tried to intervene.

#takethatrollsroyce, #fucktherich, #crazywhitepeople, were some of the nicer hashtags used.

"What do you think will happen to him?" Jenny asked, though we'd been through the different scenarios dozens of times already.

"Jail time, but not too much." Cary stated. "I'm assuming he has a clean record. Possibly he will be forced into a drug treatment center, but I doubt it. But the worst punishment will be his immediate ejection from New York society. The only people who will associate with him now are his drug dealers, and trust me, all they want is his money."

"He won't have much of that soon." I grumbled, then reached for the bottle of tequila. "I wonder when the reporters will come sniffing around?"

"Are you sure you want more liquor?" Cary whispered in my ear. Jenny must have had great hearing because she boomed out, "Drink bitch, drink!!"

I left the bottle on the table and cleared my throat. "None of us can stay here tonight. The garage is a crime scene, and the house is a disaster. Plus, we've all had too much booze. Let's reserve hotel rooms in Asheville and hire some drivers to pick us up."

"Sounds like a plan." Jenny said, then pulled out her phone and started typing.

Cary squeezed my hand and when I glanced over at him, a tear was sliding down his cheek. "I'm so sorry this happened to you."

"Hey, stop. You're the one whose fancy-ass car was destroyed." I lifted his chin with my finger and kissed the tip of his nose. "So, what's next for us?"

CHAPTER 34

CARY

"This has been the longest day of my life." Thatch yawned, then laid his head on my chest. He tightened his grip on me, and his legs were tangled with mine. We were at the Grand Bohemian Hotel, lying in bed trying to sleep, but it was next to impossible. I couldn't read his mind, but was sure Thatch was wondering what awful thing could happen next.

Me? I found it easy to let go of stupid stuff, like my demolished car, but what had happened to me, to the carefree man I'd been until I met this man who was holding me like he was terrified I'd run away?

"Thatch?" I whispered, kissing the top of his head. "Nothing prepares us for insanity. We just need to focus on the future, and eventually we'll look back on today and wonder how on earth we survived it. Though I'm wondering if perhaps this was all my fault."

"Don't go there, Cary." Thatch's grip tightened even more. "You had nothing to do with—"

"Yes, I did. If Sam hadn't brought me to your house, none of this would've happened. You might have had a strange relationship with Brian, but I doubt he'd be sitting in jail if he hadn't felt threatened by me." I tried to laugh, because the thought of me threatening anyone was absurd, but I made more of a choking sound. Tears threatened to spill when I thought of this question, but it was one that needed answering. "Is Brian still in love with you?"

"No, God, no. Brian is only in love with money, and since I was his primary source of income, he lashed out at you. You want to know why?" Thatch asked, then turned his head so I could stare down at his face. "I believe he sensed how I feel about you. We might not be married anymore, but after so many years of being in each other's lives, we can sense what's going on. It's almost like ESP or something, and if he has a pesky little cocaine habit, he would want to ensure that the money kept rolling in."

I slid down the mattress, causing Thatch to grumble. Apparently, he didn't want to let me out of his arms, but I needed a little space for what I was about to say. I turned on my side to face him, and stroked his cheek. "I love you, Thatch, and it scares the hell out of me."

"Why? I mean, why does that frighten you?" His bright blue eyes filled with tears, and I felt a lump form in my throat.

"I've never felt anything like this before. At first I just thought we'd have a tumble in the sheets and I'd get it out of my system, but that only made me want you more. Then, I tried to use my logic to rationalize how I felt about you, but it was impossible. Yes, we haven't known each other for long, but we've been through so much together over the last few weeks. It's almost like we've packed a lifetime of experiences in a brief period of time." A tear slid down my cheek, and Thatch reached over and wiped it away with his thumb. "I've never had a serious relationship with anyone. Think you can teach a lifelong bachelor how this lovey-dovey stuff works?"

"Just be you, Cary. I fell for you, because of who you are. Eccentric, funny, and kind. When you reached your hand out to Brian, to help him up after he'd destroyed your car and threatened Jenny, something in my chest exploded." Thatch reached out and lightly dragged his fingertips down my side. "You're a good man, Cary, and have I mentioned you are the handsomest fella I've ever been with?"

"Now it's my turn for chest explosions." I whispered. "I always wondered what people meant when they said stuff like that. Because of you, I now know." I leaned in and brushed my lips across his. "Would you mind terribly coming back to Raleigh with me?"

"I'd love to, but I have to oversee the repairs on the property. Plus…"

"I'm afraid for you to stay here." I blurted out, and Thatch reached over and pulled me into his chest. "Brian will probably be released on a bond, or bail, whatever it is they call it. He's got a clean record, so a judge won't think twice about releasing him. I'm frightened he'll go after you."

"I've given that some thought. Tomorrow I'll call my lawyer and talk to her about having a restraining order taken out against Brian."

I opened my mouth to speak, but Thatch laid his index finger across it.

"Living in fear of Brian will not happen. I know him better than you do, and this was the first time I've ever seen him act violently." Thatch sighed, then turned on his back, and stared at the ceiling.

"Get the restraining order, but let Jenny finish the job she's started. I'll hire a security firm to keep an eye on her while the house is being repaired. She's an expert with this kind of stuff, and after what happened in the garage, I doubt Brian wants to tangle with her again. But he's had years of experience manipulating you, Thatch. I worry more about you getting hurt by your ex again. Please, come to Raleigh, at least until all this mess with Brian is settled through the legal system." I hit the mattress with the palm of my hand. "You don't even have to stay with me. You could rent a…"

"Hush your mouth, Cary." Thatch grinned. "Of course, I'd stay with you." He sighed, then took my hand and held it to his chest. "Let's get some sleep, and tomorrow we'll do what we have to do before hitting the road. And, yes, I'll come to Raleigh. No matter where you are, I want to be there next to you."

———

The next morning, I was in the bathroom when I thought I heard a knock at the hotel room door. A moment later, I heard muffled voices, then there was a knock at the bathroom door.

"Yes?"

"Jenny must have called Dr. Creighton. She and Joey are here to make sure you're healthy enough to travel, so make sure you're decent when you come out." Thatch said. I had just gotten out of the shower, and all I had to wear was the fluffy white robe the hotel provided. I put it on and walked out to meet them.

"Dr. Creighton, it's lovely to see you again." I grinned at her, noting with pleasure she was wearing the pearls I'd given her. Joey looked a little put out, like he didn't want to be here. He wouldn't meet my gaze, and that's when I remembered he'd gone on a date with Thatch. Poor kid must have a crush on him. "Joey, good to see you too."

"You are all over the news, Mr. Lancaster. When I saw the

video of that man destroying your car, I immediately tried to get in touch with you, but none of my calls seem to have gotten through." She placed her doctor's bag on a table, and gestured toward the bed. "Have a seat, and we'll see how you are doing. Open your robe enough so I can listen to your heart."

Though I doubted I would fail this physical, I didn't want to take any chances. "Thatch, would you mind running down to Jenny's room, and…"

A knock at the door interrupted me. Thatch crossed the room and opened it. Jenny, Sam, and Celia Mae stood there with goofy grins on their faces. "Morning y'all." Celia Mae breezed in and sat on the bed next to me. "I didn't know you'd have company. Want to join us for breakfast? After that I've got to hit the road. There's some emergency at the hospital, and my boss called me in."

"You work in a hospital around here?" Dr. Creighton asked, then blew on the end of the stethoscope to warm it up.

"Oh, no. I'm an administrator at Duke University Hospital in Durham. Told my boss I'd be there by two, so I need to eat and get going." Celia Mae smiled, and I realized she and Thatch had almost identical grins.

"Looks like I might be seeing more of you." Joey crossed his arms over his chest. "I just accepted a position there, working as a surgical assistant." He glanced over to Dr. Creighton. "They offered me a lot more money."

"Not surprised." She replied, shaking her head.

"Really? Well, I'll be seeing you quite often." Celia Mae smiled at Joey. "There are several of us admins running around, but my office is next to one of the primary operating theaters. Most of my work is scheduling, so if you ever need a day off or something, just give me a holler."

"I'm sorry to do this, but would all of you mind leaving the room, so I can examine Mr. Lancaster?" Dr. Creighton asked.

"He can meet you for breakfast in a few minutes. He's looking much better, so I'm sure this will be a brief visit."

"Oh, sure." Thatch reached over and ruffled my hair. "We'll be downstairs in the hotel restaurant."

"Actually, I won't." Sam walked to the door and opened it. "I'm going to visit Dad. If he'll see me, that is."

"Why on earth do you want to see him?" Jenny asked with a pinched look on her face. I loved the woman like a sister, but sometimes she could be a little dense when it came to emotions.

"Jenny, it's his father." I murmured, and she shrugged her shoulders.

"Don't be long, cause I've got to leave right after we're done eating." Celia Mae walked over to Sam and kissed his forehead. "And, be careful. I know you love him, but his head's not in a good place right now."

"I'm driving to Durham this afternoon, around one o'clock to look at some apartments. If you want, I can give you a lift." Joey offered, and Sam's face brightened a little.

"Really? That would be awesome. Just meet me here, I guess." Sam grinned, then glanced over to Thatch, and his smile faltered. "Dad, I'm sorry about..."

"None of this is your fault, Sam. Well, except for you introducing me to Cary, and I'm not holding that against you." Thatch walked over to his son, and wrapped his arms around him. "I love you, Sam. Never forget that. C'mon, we'll walk out with you."

Moments later, it was just me, the doctor, and Joey. She grinned down at me, then said, "Bet you expected none of this to happen."

CHAPTER 35

THATCH

Two days later and Brian was out of jail. We learned about it on CNN, who'd been following the case since the videos of Brian's meltdown went viral. To my dismay, he sent Sam a message letting him know he would be at the house in Nags Head. He wasn't allowed to leave the state, and didn't want to risk being seen by the news media currently parked outside our house.

"That's the last of your stuff from the office." Jenny handed me a large cardboard box, and I squeezed it into the last remaining space in the back of my SUV. There was a smudge on her forehead, and Cary rubbed it away with his finger. "Oh, and while I was packing, I got a message from the attorney I hired. The restraining order is now in place. This restricts him from being within five hundred yards of both of you. May I make a recommendation?"

"Yes, please." I replied, having discovered over the last few days that this woman was possibly the most organized and effective person I'd ever met.

"Rest for a couple of days, but then I'd hightail it up to New

York and get your belongings out of your apartment there. Brian can't leave the state, and this is an excellent window of opportunity for you to tie up loose ends in the city."

"I know an excellent realtor." Cary slung his arm over my shoulders. "Put the apartment on sale as soon as possible. This place—" He gestured toward the house, "—should be ready for a realtor within a couple of weeks, I think."

Jenny nodded her agreement. "The cleanup is mostly done. Now it's about scheduling repairs. Getting contractors to show up and do the work is a pain in the ass."

"How long do you think you'll be here?" Cary asked, and I realized I was taking his assistant away from her duties.

"Jenny doesn't have to..." I started, but Jenny cut me off.

"I work for Cary, and I will stay here for as long as it takes to get things done." She grinned, then stood on her tiptoes and kissed my cheek. "Allow me to take care of this mess. It's what I do best, and the two of you have been through enough already. Now, scoot. I've got work to do."

She pecked Cary on the cheek. "Bye, boss, Love you." Then, she skipped back into the garage.

I glanced up at the house, and memories flooded my head. Brian and I had built it, the house of our dreams where we'd raise Sam, and hopefully be able to retire, but now he was out of the picture, and my dreams and goals had changed.

"Everything I wanted was once here, in this house. I'm going to miss it." I swiped at my eyes. "Where was the butterfly when it flapped its wings?"

"Huh?" Cary squinted at me.

"You know, that thing from chaos theory. A butterfly, or something similar, flaps its wings on the other side of the world, and it creates unexpected changes around the globe. Like, triggering a tornado in North Carolina, or thrusting two people into each other's lives, who probably would never have met without a little cosmic nudge." I sighed, and Cary smacked my ass.

"Hey, what was that for?"

Cary turned, placed his forehead against mine, and whispered, "Don't get so deep in your head. Just embrace change, and live in the moment."

———

"Welcome to my new home. I only moved in a few weeks before we met, so it's still kind of empty." Cary said, then the elevator doors opened, and he gestured for me to walk in first. It was the penthouse, and through sliding glass doors on the opposite side of the living room, I could see a deck with a small pool. Aside from a weathered leather couch and a coffee table, there wasn't much to see. No pictures on the white walls, no personal knick-knacks, either. I placed the box I was holding on the floor, and noticed a light echo as I did.

"You weren't kidding. It's practically empty."

"It's odd, but I've never been good at holding onto things. After my folks died, I donated most of their stuff to charity. They had thousands of books, and I know you hate to hear this, but they would've just gathered dust if I'd kept them." Cary placed his arm around my waist and pulled me in close. "I think it's because I didn't have anyone I wanted to set up housekeeping with. Like, what was the point in accumulating stuff if none of it meant much to me?"

"I'm the opposite. For most of my life, I've been a packrat, but now I want a clean break from the past." I kissed Cary's stubbled cheek, then disengaged from him, and strolled around the apartment, with him following a few steps behind.

"It's rented, so if you don't like it, we can always..."

I spun around, a huge smile splitting my face. "We. You said we, like you really meant it."

"Of course, I did, because I do." Cary smiled back at me. "We are at the beginning of something special. I can feel it in my heart. Your happiness means the world to me, so if you aren't in love with this place, we can go wherever you want. I'm mostly retired now. The art gallery project has been on the back burner the last few weeks, because of, well, you know."

I giggled. "Yeah, I can see why."

"The gallery was a heart project, something I've always wanted to do. I want to discover new artists and help them succeed. If not in Raleigh, I can do it wherever else we may end up." Cary said, then turned down a hallway. The walls were painted a brilliant red, and there were a couple of portraits hung. "My parents," he pointed at them, and kept on walking. At the end of the hall, he opened a door, and a giant antique wooden bed filled the center of the room. "This is the only room I've decorated."

"It's beautiful." I murmured, and meant it. Dozens of paintings and photographs dotted the pale blue walls, and stunning bamboo blinds covered the windows. It had a European flair I hadn't seen outside of Paris. "This is how I imagined your home."

"Now that you're here, it will finally feel like a home, not a place I just sleep in." Cary wrapped his arms around me from behind, and kissed the back of my neck. "Just remember, the most important thing is us—not things, or homes, or money—us."

I slowly turned, not wanting him to let go of his embrace. He intuitively held on to me. When I faced him, I kissed his forehead, then the tip of his nose, and finally his full, wet lips.

"I love you, Cary."

"And I love you, Thatch. More than I ever dreamed was possible."

EPILOGUE
JENNY- TWO YEARS LATER

"Cary, I just saw Brian through the windows."

He swiveled his head to see if he could spot him. When he did he frowned. "Jesus, the man won't give up, bless his heart." Cary pursed his lips. "I love that saying. Bless your heart. So polite, yet cutting at the same time."

"Thatch is definitely rubbing off on you," I grinned. "In more ways than one. Now, back to the problem at hand. He's outside the bookstore, so Brian is violating the restraining order, but he hasn't tried to enter… Yet."

We were at the Strand bookstore in Manhattan. Thatch was giving a lecture followed by a book signing, and then he had an appointment with the realtor to finalize the sale of his and Brian's old apartment. Because of the restraining order, Brian could not attend the closing. He'd bitched through his lawyers, but even he wasn't stupid enough to stop the sale. Stupid druggie needed the cash.

"What does Luis think?" Cary asked, referring to the body-guard we employed whenever we were in New York.

"Gimme a sec." I replied, then hit the button on my headset. "Luis, do you think Brian is a threat?"

A moment later, he replied, though it was difficult to hear him through the rain outside where he was monitoring the front door. "Nah, he looks exhausted, or strung out. Who knows? I'll let you know if he attempts to enter. There's a police officer here too, so if he tries, I'll ask him to assist."

"Luis doesn't believe Brian will come inside, but there is a police officer outside who can help if he tries to enter." I said, and noticed a remorseful look pass over Cary's face. Damn it, he always felt sorry for Brian. "Stop it right now. He destroyed your car, spat on you, and then had the nerve to sue you for defamation, when all you did was tell the truth. Cary, the man did this to himself."

"I know, but I remember the last time I saw him, and the haunted look in his eyes. Brian didn't even look like the man Thatch was married to." Cary sighed. "It's drugs, everyone knows it. If only he would get some help."

"What would help is if his so-called friends would stop giving him money, especially when they know it's all going up his nose." I shook my head, then Luis's voice filled my headset.

"Brian is gone. I still recommend exiting the building through the rear, accompanied by me and store security." Luis's voice crackled. "The event is over in fifty-two minutes. I'll be inside five minutes prior to that, unless Brian shows up again."

"Thanks, Luis."

"I want to go to California and visit Sam and Joey soon." Cary grinned, then passed his phone to me. The screen was filled with Sam's Instagram page. The two of them were standing in front of a pretty bungalow they'd just bought in West Hollywood. "Thatch spoke to them last night. Joey got a nursing job at Cedar-Sinai, and Sam is officially a screenwriter for some Netflix series. It's amazing how fate intervened to bring them together. If I hadn't been trying to score with Sam, I'd never have met Thatch. And if Joey hadn't been my nurse, he'd never have met Sam."

I handed him his phone back and rubbed his upper arm. Since Thatch and Cary had eloped to Vegas, my old boss had become a different man. Like, sentimental to the point of making me nauseous, and, oh my God, the PDA between him and Thatch was revolting. But, he had never been so happy, and that was what was important.

Applause filled the room, and I glanced over to where Thatch stood behind a lectern. A broad, toothy smile flashed across his face as he faced his fans. His latest book was flying off the shelves, and part of that success was made possible by Cary.

In the past, Thatch had done next to zero publicity whenever he launched a novel. Cary had convinced him that meeting his readers would send his sales through the roof, because of his earthy and warm personality. He'd also insisted on Thatch giving lectures about the writing process, and on topical matters currently in the news. He figured that since most of Thatch's books were inspired by current events, why not capitalize on that and brand himself as an expert. As a result, Thatch made the rounds of cable news shows, as well as the silly morning programs. Viewers loved him and his southern schtick, and he was rapidly becoming a household name.

"So, when are you going to fess up with what's going on between you and Celia Mae?" Cary whispered, and when I faced him, I recognized the rakish gleam in his eyes that I rarely saw anymore.

"It's nothing serious." I bit my lower lip at the tiny lie. "We're having fun, that's all."

"Uh huh." Cary winked.

Both Celia Mae and I had wanted to keep our affair a secret, but Sam had walked in on us one evening at the apartment in Raleigh. We'd been house-sitting while Thatch and Cary were vacationing in Mexico, and Sam had thought the place would be empty. Instead, he experienced the shock of seeing first hand just how kinky his aunt really was. Neither of us were into women that much, but there was something between us I couldn't explain. She was a strong, sexy woman, and when we finally hooked up, our sexual chemistry was pure dynamite. Sam promised to keep quiet, but we knew he'd spill the beans eventually.

"Is that why she's suddenly accompanying us to all these events?" Cary winked, and I glanced over to the far side of the room where Celia Mae was leaning against the wall staring straight at me. I licked my lips, and she did the same, but slower. Blood inched up my neck, and I deliberately looked away to keep from getting too flustered.

"She put in her years at the hospital, and now that she's retired, Celia Mae wants to travel, that's all." Jesus, Cary was like a dog with a bone. Ever since he'd gotten married, he was determined everyone else should be, too. I couldn't see myself getting married to anyone, ever, but shacking up with Celia Mae Fuller wasn't such a bad idea.

Applause roared through the room again, and Cary and I turned and faced Thatch behind the podium.

"I only have time for one more question." He drawled, then pointed at a short, pink-haired woman with glasses wearing a pride t-shirt. "Ask me anything."

"Mr. Fuller, it is such an honor to meet you." The young woman's voice was breathy and light, making it hard to understand. "What motivates you? I mean, if you had to name one thing that drives you to write such incredible stories, what would that be?"

Thatch dipped his head for a moment, and I could see him

biting his lower lip, then he straightened up, grinned, and pointed across the room to where we were standing.

"My husband, Cary, whom I love very much. He changed my life, and now he is my muse."

———

Thank you for reading Cary and Thatch's love story. It was fun to write, and I hope you enjoyed it. The next book in the Southern Discomfort series is called Inconveniently Yours. Here's the blurb.

"Swear to God, his nose is so high in the air he could drown in a rainstorm."

Chase is a country boy living the dream, though most

people would call it a nightmare. He's the personal assistant to the vice-president of a global conglomerate, a man so cold you'll be forgiven for thinking ice water flows through his veins. When he first meets his boss he is smitten by him, but after three years of what can only be called low-paid slavery, he's had enough. On the verge of quitting, disaster strikes, and Chase finally discovers a way to climb the corporate ladder. Unfortunately for him, that means marrying the boss.

Everyone loathes Juan, and he doesn't give a damn. His only desire is to succeed, and he doesn't care who he steps on to achieve his goals. When it's discovered he has violated the terms of his visa, he's threatened with deportation. Juan will do anything to stay in the United States, and not lose his powerful and lucrative job. Panicked, he tells the board of directors he's marrying his assistant, Chase, who promptly blackmails Juan into promoting him. Unable to say no, the two embark on a road trip to meet Chase's eccentric southern family, and end up discovering there's more between them than they've ever thought possible.

Inconveniently Yours is the second book in the Southern Discomfort series. Prepare yourself for sweet tea and sour words, served alongside men discovering their deepest desires. Inconveniently Yours has it all; enemies to lovers, a fake relationship, and two men falling in love for the first time. So relax on your porch swing with a mint julep and a slice of pecan pie, and enjoy the journey to true love.

ACKNOWLEDGMENTS

Thanks to my editor Ann Attwood who does a fabulous job of keeping me on track. I'd also like to thank my friend Victor Hugo, who keeps me mellowed out.

ABOUT THE AUTHOR

Ian O. Lewis is a bestselling author of LGBTQ romance and fiction. He's from the American south, but currently lives in Mexico. Follow him on Amazon, Bookbub, and social media to stay up to date with his life and new releases.

ALSO BY IAN O. LEWIS

The Boys of Oregon Hill Series

Lovefool

Recreational Love

Mr. Mouthful

Handsy

The Boundary

The Making It Series

Making It Spark

Making It Sizzle

Making It Glitter

Making It Legal

The Balcony Boys Series

Situationship

Max

The Men of Hidden Creek Series

Serve

Missionary (A Standalone Novel)

CPSIA information can be obtained
at www.ICGtesting.com
Printed in the USA
BVHW091740140622
639736BV00013B/1211